INVOLVEMENT IN AUSTRIA

INVOLVEMENT
IN AUSTRIA

John Newton Chance

Chivers Press • G.K. Hall & Co.
Bath, England   Thorndike, Maine USA

This Large Print edition is published by Chivers Press, England, and by G.K. Hall & Co., USA.

Published in 1998 in the U.K. by arrangement with Robert Hale Ltd.

Published in 1998 in the U.S. by arrangement with Robert Hale Ltd.

U.K. Hardcover ISBN 0–7540–3181–0 (Chivers Large Print)
U.K. Softcover   ISBN 0–7540–3182–9 (Camden Large Print)
U.S. Softcover   ISBN 0–7838–8406–0 (Nightingale Series Edition)

Copyright © John Newton Chance 1969

The text of this Large Print edition is unabridged.
Other aspects of the book may vary from the original edition.

Set in 16 pt. New Times Roman.

Printed in Great Britain on acid-free paper.

British Library Cataloguing in Publication Data available

Library of Congress Catalog Card Number: 97-94861
ISBN: 0-7838-8406-0 (lg. print : sc)

CHAPTER ONE

One summer, about dusk, I was driving fast along an empty road when a hole appeared in the windscreen not far from my head. In my kind of past I have seen such holes before. They are made by bullets.

Ahead of me the dark green trees of a forest showed, but to either side of the road there was open ground, and nowhere for a body to hide and fire a shot at me.

In the mirror I saw a car—or part of the back of it—formating on my port rear quarter.

Another hole came.

I trod down hard, and went ahead and I saw the beetle shape of a Porsche with something sticking out of the window very clearly shown in my mirror.

I went right ahead, but he started to come up again. It was unpleasant. I didn't seem to hear any noise of the cars or the wind. It was as if this death chase took place in a dream.

Then from somewhere over on my right I heard the bellow of the air horns on a Diesel train, and with that, sound of the race came back to my half-frozen brain.

Not far ahead there was a slip round, a right turn that could just be made at speed if the shoulder of the road was hard on the far side.

I turned suddenly and braked together. She

1

held it screaming. For one moment it did seem that she would heel too far and go over, for that turn was no fair test for any car.

What saved us was the road shoulder, which was hard and rose a bit, so we stopped the heeling and bumped over upright. It got me round into the narrow road running towards the fringe of the forest trees.

In the glass I just saw the Porsche flash past, stop lights blazing. A third hole joined the others in my back window but went out of the left side one behind me. I got going really fast.

The air horns of the Diesel sounded again. I glanced right and a way off the train showed, its long line of windows yellow glowing against the purple evening.

My road was heading straight towards the tracks, but I saw no crossing gates until I rounded a bend.

I remember seeing a sign that bawled 'Achtung!' and somewhat else, but my whole attention was riveted on the vertical poles of the crossing.

They shivered as if the mechanism was just going into action. The train was about a half mile off on my right, its headlights burning up the dusk now. The air horns went again.

The poles started to come down. I trod on the last horse in the box and shot under the bars as they came down.

That is, I shot under one and clipped the other with the roof. It was a hell of a clip and

2

sent the pole slightly upwards with the reaction.

I thought it would stop me right on the crossing with the train headlight, a mile high it seemed, blaring down on me like the eyes of hell.

The air horns blew so my ears rang and I could hear nothing else.

But the car went under the second pole, which screeched on the rear of the roof. I went on, with nothing but the roar and clatter of the train behind me and the dying wail of the air horns blasting away into the distance.

I felt like an old film, well spotted.

The road was narrow and wound round through the firs. I spared a moment for the dial marked 'Gas'. The needle was stuck to the bottom and not shifting even in hope.

I had meant to fill up at the frontier two kilometres from where the road had turned off. I hoped—faintly—that the gauge was not reliable, for you never know with hired cars and it did seem to have used overmuch for the mileage done.

But there wasn't much time to think. I had no lights on then. It seemed best not to. Behind me headlights glared and flashed and jazzed through the straight trunks of the firs.

Ahead of me there was a track forking off into the wilderness. With no petrol but hope left, it was the only thing to do. To keep on the road was to get caught up and done up.

I went on to the track and in a moment the

lights of the pursuing car were almost lost as the growing barrier of the trees thickened up between us.

The engine faded. I steered off the track and down soft needle-covered slopes until I was deep in the undergrowth.

I got out and ran back up the slope until I was on the track again. Flickering between the distant trees I saw the glow of headlights, running hard away into the distance.

I wiped my face, and then had a cigarette and tried to think what the hell it was all about.

In Austria I knew nobody. In fact, I hadn't meant to be there. I had started off on a holiday without any set heading, as I usually do. I like to think I surprise myself with where I end up.

I hired the Mercedes in Koln four days back, and Koln was a good long way back now. I had just headed on and on, going East to wherever they would look at my passport. I was running out of such friendly organisation now. I could almost smell the cold iron of the curtain.

So I knew nobody. I couldn't think of any old friends suddenly spotting me driving across middle Europe and then deciding to blow me off my seat because of some past irritation.

It must have been a mistake. I had been mistaken for somebody else, though why, with a German registration plate, I couldn't work out. Had I been just an ordinary tourist, with no experience of having been shot at before, I

4

should have been surprised, then indignant, then dead before I had any chance of knowing what it was all about.

But whoever I had been mistaken for must have been a very much wanted character. I hoped that the mistake had been due to the car and not to any physical resemblance of myself to the pursued one.

I realised that running away might have the guilty look to those behind. They would probably think that an innocent bystander would at once have pulled up and they could then have apologised to his corpse.

The forest was silent then, all trains and cars having faded into the distant quiet. It was also dark and getting darker.

There I was in the middle of a dark nowhere with a useless car, cigarettes and nothing else. It could be a damn long walk to anywhere, providing I guessed the right way to go.

Eastward, I knew, lay the frontier. I also knew they wouldn't let me through, so it meant retracing steps.

Back to where the Porsche-load of death was keeping a lookout. It was hardly worth taking the risk that they might realise their mistake and go away.

The possibility was that I might resemble the guy they were looking for and they didn't waste much time asking questions about it.

The last place I had stopped was about five for grub and cigarettes. It was not a busy day.

Apart from a fat blonde who served and took the money, there had been no other guests there but me.

The ride from there, apart from a few lorry trains and buses, had been surprisingly quiet. It seemed that few private motorists wanted to get behind the iron.

Remembering the journey back to that meal did no good at all. I hadn't noticed being tailed, and as I normally use the mirror regularly several times a minute, it was pretty certain the Porsche had come out from some side road or layby and come up fast behind me.

In fact, as I had not seen it until the first shot cracked the windscreen, it must have come up from the wrong side of the road.

Whatever it had done it had mercifully gone and my present need was to find where I was and get help out of it.

I went back to the car and got the torch out, also a map. But the map was too small a scale to help in this case.

The forest was an angular green splodge and the road I had crossed the railway tracks by wasn't even marked.

A long way south of where I appeared to be was a *schloss* but that could be a ruin.

Back on the track I used the next position; which is to see if the track is used. There were marks of tyres here and there cast in when the road had been muddy. At the sides I also saw marks where vehicles had driven in close, corresponding marks on the other side of the track showed that vehicles passed here and there.

Which indicated that the track went somewhere. It was worth trying. Very soon I was to wish I hadn't.

As I started to walk south along it, I had the feeling I was being too nervous about going on to the frontier post. I couldn't very well be shot right in front of the officials clamouring around there.

Or could I?

It was that small doubt that kept me on the track until I saw a light through the trees ahead. I felt like one of the lost children in the forest who suddenly saw the lights of the gingerbread house.

The witch's place. Remember?

The track widened out and came round to the back of a large, ornate sort of hunting lodge of the old days, when the reigning prince would put up forty guests and fifty servants as a change from roughing it back in the palace in Vienna.

The carved external woodwork was a fascinating feature to one once a surveyor. I even began to try and work out a price for such work today as a relief from worrying about why somebody nearly shot me.

I was coming in to a stabling yard. As I went into it a man came towards me, a big, lurking, hulking figure in the dusk.

From the light streaming from an open doorway I saw he held a sporting gun pointing at me and it looked as if he had both barrels cocked.

'Halt!' he snorted, and rolled off into a string of German which didn't appeal to me.

'I speak only English,' I said.

'So,' he said, and nodded. 'Pig.'

'Please yourself,' I said. 'I might be the goddam pig who got up and walked away.'

'What do you talk of? What's your name?'

'Blake,' I said. 'What's yours?'

'It will not interest you,' he said.

'Just for the record,' I said.

'Get in that door,' he said, jerking the gun at the opening.

'I've come here for some help,' I said. 'That's all. Not to help myself.'

It was a simple test to see how much vernacular he did know. He laughed, so he knew that much.

I went in at the door. For a back door it was massive but he poked the gun in my back and forced me past before I could appreciate the workmanship.

A fine, plump blonde girl stood at the end of the big passage, a pair of plaits hanging over her voluminous bust. She looked just curious; not surprised, but just curious, as if prisoners were brought in by the dozen every day.

I smiled at her and she smiled back, eagerly, almost. Well, I had one possible friend, I

8

thought as the man shoved me past her with the gun.

'Who is it, Jacob?' she said.

'Blake,' I said, half turning to her.

'Get on,' Jacob said, shoving the gun hard.

It hurt. As I turned back to go on I hooked the barrel with my elbow and kept on swinging right round, away from any possible shot and thudded him right in the nose as he fired.

Both barrels, I noticed.

A large lump of plaster burst from the wall and sprayed over the floor in dust and lumps. The sound of the shots was like a small cannon in there.

He still held the gun as he staggered around, trying to work out what had happened. I wrenched it away from him and he fell up against the wall, shaking his head.

The girl burst into a little scream of laughter.

Jacob stood away from the wall. I gave him the gun back.

'I don't like being prodded,' I said.

'Himmel!' he grunted, and wiped his bleeding nose.

2

'Get on!' he said, when he had got his sense back. 'Go! Forward!'

'Let him stay a minute,' the girl said. 'There is no hurry. The Countess is in the bath.'

Jacob was mopping his nose again.

'Go and fix your nose,' the girl said. 'He

9

won't go. I will look after him. Fix your nose. Blood makes her mad.'

Their dialogue took place in German, but I got most of it. He stood the empty gun against the wall and shambled off and went into a room near the back door.

'He means well, for what he is supposed to do,' the girl said, smiling. 'But he is very stupid as you see.'

'Why go for me with a gun?' I asked. 'I came merely because my car ran out of gas.'

I made no remark on the fact that she spoke to me direct in English, as if she had heard what I had said to Jacob out in the stabling yard.

'The Countess must meet everybody,' the girl said. 'No one comes that she does not see. It is the rule, you see.'

'At gun point?'

She chuckled.

'That is just Jacob's way,' she said. 'He is very stupid if he has no gun.'

'He seems pretty stupid with one,' I said. 'What's your name?'

'Anna.'

'Well, Anna, is there any gas here? That's all I came for.'

'I would not know,' she said and shrugged so that her plaits swung.

Bells started ringing furiously. Anna stared and looked away down to a bend in the passage.

10

'It is her,' she said. 'You must come now!'

She seemed quite breathless from the sudden command of the bells. The Countess seemed to have some considerable influence, to say the least. It occurred to me that Jacob's fatheaded thrumping about with the gun was not the result of his own ideas, but trying to get approved by somebody else's.

Anna flicked the plaits over her shoulders so that they swung at her back as I followed her quick, heavy steps into the unknown.

We came into the hall, the dining hall, carousing hall, whatever hall. Black panelled, carved like a wooden Christmas tree and with a refectory table running down the middle that looked as long as a cricket pitch with candlesticks spaced up it, all alight with tall candles and places laid for twenty or thirty. I had no time to count, but the silver and glass, shining in the candlelight, was one of the richest things I have ever seen.

So was the woman who sat in the mighty carver at the head of the long, shining table.

She was very dark and wore a pair of earrings that sparkled like candelabra. At first sight she seemed very beautiful and puzzling, for I just couldn't put an age to her. Not less than twenty-five, not more than forty doesn't get far. She was as beautiful as a girl but had the quiet assurance of a woman of experience.

She wore a loose satin quilted gown and looked as if she had just stepped out of a bath

11

into it and come down to the table.

Which, I found, she had.

'Sit down,' she said.

It was a direction, not an invitation. It made me rather mad. She seemed to be playing a part of how-to-get-disliked-in-Act-One and she was spot on with it.

'You are English,' she said, stating it, not asking.

'I am Jonathan Blake. I come from Cornwall, which is attached to England and is struggling for independence. Just like me. I have the bad feeling of being a prisoner. Explain that, if you please.'

'Your feeling is right,' she said. 'You are a prisoner.'

'Who the devil are you?' I snapped at her.

'I am Catherine—' and she went on to give her names and titles which seemed to take in every territory I'd ever learnt at school as being part of the old Austro-Hungarian empire.

It made me feel I was drifting into a world of 1880.

But perhaps one got shot at just as often then.

In fact, with all those counts and dukes about, probably more often.

'Well, that's very interesting,' I said. 'I am glad to meet you, because you are obviously worth meeting. Even without that library of names. But your presumption I just won't have. I am nobody's prisoner.'

12

'I have a guard here who is sure you will be mine,' she said.

I took out a cigarette and lit it. It was rude. It was meant to be.

'Do you, by any chance, own a carload of thugs firing out of the windows at passers by?'

She cocked her head. The earrings swung in sparkling agitation, and then were still.

'You were shot at?' she said.

'I was. Murderously.'

'Where?'

I told her—as nearly as I could.

'What make of car?'

'A Porsche. Two tone grey. Saloon, that is, fixed top. I think there were three men. I was busy ducking bullets and am not therefore very sure.'

'You saw no number?'

'I have told you all I did see. Three shots were fired. All hit my car at window level and came inside one way or another. The marksman, therefore, had had experience.'

'How did you escape?'

I told her about it.

'Now I want petrol,' I said, 'and will be on my way.'

She looked askance. The earrings danced again.

'One would have thought you would wish to telephone the police.'

'I never quite know the ploy in foreign lands,' I said. 'There was a time when I went to

13

the gendarmes to get protection from a certain party, only to find the chief of police was in the pay of the same party.'

She smiled ironically.

'So this is not the first time that you have been shot at?' she said.

'I should say it's about the forty-ninth,' I said.

'What are you, then?'

'I am Jonathan Blake. That is English for One Who Gets Involved. I can't turn a corner without meeting with somebody who involves me in something.'

'But when you are shot at, what did you do the other times?'

'Shot back,' I said.

She watched me and took a gold-tipped cigarette from a box on the table. This time I unbent slightly and flicked my lighter for her. The reek of Turkish swept across me before she said anything more.

'You shot back,' she said. 'You carry a gun?'

'I don't at the moment. I find carrying guns in foreign countries something of an open invitation to the clink. So it is at home, of course.'

'But not for you?'

'I have a licence, certificate, permit—what do you call it here? Anyway the police approve me. I belong to a Pistol Club.'

'Yet you shoot at people?'

'If they shoot at me. Yes.'

14

'You would have shot back tonight?'

'Certainly.'

She thought about that, smoking quietly and watching me. I kept my eyes open, too, for I had the feeling that we were being watched yet there appeared to be no one in the big hall but ourselves.

'Where does the road go?' I said. 'The one they took after me?'

'It goes to Krin. A village on the frontier. The guards there are more obliging than those on the main roads. A good deal of smuggling goes on through there.'

'So they'll feel at home,' I said. 'You seem very interested in these people. Do you know who they are?'

She shrugged then and the gown slipped almost off one shoulder. I was right. She had come straight out of the bath.

'Near the frontier you get many factions, many gangs,' she said. 'For all I know, you could be involved.'

'I came to Austria just for the ride,' I said. 'I'm on holiday. I have no commitments.'

'You came alone?'

'Yes.'

'Married?'

'I have no legal involvements. How about you?'

'Have you thought what would happen if these men came?'

'No. I don't make myself miserable for the

15

sake of it.'

'But they can't let you go,' she said. 'You can witness that they are murderers, or mean to be.'

'As I say, I don't know how important that is to your police,' I said.

'It is quite important. And to the Security, very important. If they come—' she seemed to savour the possibility, like tasting wine, '—they will kill you, will they not?'

'They will not if I see them first,' I said.

'I do not want it to happen here, for personal reasons,' she said, stubbing out a partly smoked cigarette.

'My reasons are personal, too,' I said. 'But yours must be slightly different. You said you had a guard here.'

'I do not want a war—yet.'

'Yet? What does it matter when? If any time, why not now?' I laughed then because it seemed the only thing to do. She was so dead serious and yet said things I would have thought belonged in a comic.

I was damned wrong at that, but you can't always get the angle at the start. Quite frankly at this point I got no angle at all.

A lovely lady, presumably the boss, and therefore alone, I guessed, for she needed a guard.

Guards, also presumably, are armed with something or they aren't much good in this kind of forest setting. Anyhow, Jacob had

16

already bolted me up with a gun, so there was probably more than one lying around.

And a war. She did not want her guards involved in any fighting. That was, not at that time. Not yet. Which meant that a war was planned for them at some time in the future.

If I hadn't been shot at I would have pursued this comic strip theme, but I had been, so it wasn't all as funny as I hoped to make out.

'I don't understand why you should be so flippant when you are about to be murdered,' she said.

'It's the only time one can afford to be. Tell me about your war. Is it to do with these gentlemen who have such an interest in me?'

'That I could not say,' she said, and then became quite open for a while. 'I do not know just who will be concerned. Ours will be defensive, you understand.'

'You always lose defensive wars,' I said. 'Take a lesson from the English. They only turn offensive after they have lost.'

She shrugged. The gown slipped a little more. She rang a bell and nothing appeared to happen. But after a while a girl came in, a tall dark girl in jeans and open-necked white shirt. She carried a silver tray with wine and glasses.

She didn't say a word but she looked at me, apparently so briefly, but so penetratingly that I felt I had been photographed for future reference.

Catherine poured wine and gave me a glass.

17

It was good. It made me feel better, but my head must have been in a muzz then by being shot at, disturbed by wanting to know what this set-up was, and yet I found myself taking small interested bets on when the gown was going to fall off the shoulder altogether.

She proposed a toast I didn't understand. We drank.

'You must drink it all, each time,' she said.

So we did. She kept on proposing toasts which I didn't understand. The glasses flashed, empty, full, empty, full.

'I am Catherine—' and she went on with the whole list again.

She must be drunk, I thought. Or perhaps she has been all the time.

She got up suddenly, pushing the chair back. She turned and walked away from me.

'Come,' she said.

I went. I wanted to see round the place. We went out of the hall into a broad black wooden corridor and then in at a great double door as high as a film set.

It was a bedroom of gilt magnificence, the pride of the You-know-what-bergs no doubt.

She kept her back to me. The gown slipped. Right off.

She was ready to get back in the bath.

CHAPTER TWO

1

The scene was astonishing, exciting, encouraging. Following a naked girl across her bedroom is, I suppose, all of these things on most predictable occasions.

But here, there was a difference.

There were four other girls sitting around, watching me, not Catherine.

They were all in jeans and white shirts open at the neck. They were all fine, big girls, much of a size, as if picked for their matching qualities.

Each one sat in a casual attitude, as if the scene were only of mild interest.

But each one had an automatic—Luger looking from the distance—in her lap, each hand idly touching each butt.

I do not count myself as knowledgable in matters of mid-European etiquette, but even so this lay-out looked tautly unpleasant to me.

It did not need super intelligence to realise that this was the guard, or part of it. A monstrous regiment of women. Unlike the fat, giggling blonde with the plaits I had met first, this was a tough consignment by any standards.

Catherine went through an open doorway by the head of the vast satin and gold bed. I stopped where I was because I thought that was the intention of the silent watchers. I didn't want to upset them at this early stage. I had been upset enough already out on the highway.

From this range those girls couldn't miss, even if three out of the four were rotten shots.

Catherine went out of sight into the bathroom, but started talking. I sat sat on the bed and took a smoke. The girls stayed relaxed and quite still.

'It is possible,' she said, 'that what you have done in the past has attracted the shots.'

'Not here,' I said. 'I told you, I know no one.'

'Did you know anyone where you hired the car?'

'Yes, I know Koln pretty well. But only to be friendly. Nothing has ever happened to me in Germany. My visits have been casual, as this one is now. It must be a case of a mistake.'

The girls stayed still, motionless and emotionless. It was like trying to unpersuade a jury with its mind made up. I began to feel the back of my neck crawling with increasing fear.

Of all the things that seem frightening in nature a dead, cold woman is about the worst.

'It is possible the car came from across the border,' Catherine said.

'That would be even more remote from my affairs,' I said.

'Political affairs are far reaching.'

'I am not politically minded.'

'You must have some views.'

'Indeed. But they are more inclined to sacking all parties, all politicians and putting in

20

men who know how to run a business. It's the only hope.'

'So you have views.'

'I would hardly call them political.'

'But they choose private enterprise as against socialist control,' Catherine said.

'That would be stretching it.'

'Reds do stretch these things. Anything not for Communism is against it and must be destroyed.'

'Our economy is not quite so violent at home.'

'You cannot tell what goes on underneath.'

'I still say no political firebrand would care a damn about me.'

'But you have enemies?'

'I don't regard them as such, but they might be.'

'Some, perhaps, who would pay to have you rubbed out, as they say?'

'I hadn't thought of it. Now that I do, I don't recall anyone in particular who might lay out a large sum for my funeral.'

'It must be painful to keep joking about such a subject,' she said.

'I find it soothing. Taking it seriously is likely to be disturbing. I don't like tensions. That is the road to darkest Dyspepsia.'

She came out wearing a white shirt and riding breeches. She sat on a gilt chair by the bed and one of the girls came over and put on her riding boots for her. Catherine looked well

21

used to being waited on hand and foot.

'You ride?' Catherine said.

'I have done so, but am inclined to fall off.'

'The ground is soft here.'

'I hope so.'

Riding in the dark in a thick forest was likely to be very different from the idle hacking across the Cornish moors which was about all the riding I had done till then.

'What's the point of riding this time of night?' I said.

She ignored me and gave some orders to the girls. Nobody moved so I thought they were instructions for the future, or in-the-event-of, type of advice.

My understanding of German is all right if it spoken slowly, clearly and in accordance with the rules of grammar. When quick and full of idioms and local name stuff I get lost. I got lost then.

At the start I sensed a warning about somebody coming and if they did then—it went on to say what while I was still trying to untie the beginning.

One thing she had said stayed in my mind then as a subject for thought: that the murderers might have come from beyond the curtain.

What I had told her was only a part of the story because I saw no point in telling her everything. But in fact, some months before I had been involved in sorting out an agent-

22

transporting system.

We had sorted it out enough for the security bods to move in and stop up the escape holes. It needed no very sharp brain to guess against what political organisations this move had been directed. Today the political fence has two sides and no shades. You're either red or blue, no purples.

But I had been only a tool of the security forces who needed a dumbbell to get involved and find things out that way. I really couldn't think that a consortium of nations beyond the screen could have been incensed by my behaviour so as to need my evaporation.

Except that—I realised it with a faint shock—as I got nearer the frontier they might have thought I was at it again.

Catherine named the girls for me. Trudi, a blonde with long hair done up tightly with a bun behind; Freddie, who had short black hair; Eva, a redhead with chrysanthemum cut, and a light brown mop of straight hair, name of Brigette. They did not acknowledge their names but kept watching me.

Eva, the redhead, had green eyes like a cat's, the three others had blue eyes. They all watched steadily, coldly, as if considering which part of me to shoot at first.

Anna came in, flaxen plaits swinging.

'Jacob has the horses ready,' she said.

She stood aside as Catherine walked straight by and out of the corridor. Eva nodded to me

23

to follow, so I did.

Catherine did not mind my following her where she could not see me, for Eva and Trudi came up right behind me.

We went through the hall and along the corridors by which I had come in. As we came out to the yard I heard restless horses' shoes clattering the cobbles, eager to go.

There were four horses. Eva helped Catherine up on to a big bay and signed me to a chestnut beside it. Jacob held both horses' heads and mine was tugging upwards to break the control.

There is nothing like riding a mettlesome horse in loose flannel trousers to flay the skin off the inside of your calves. I wasn't looking forward to it.

Eva and Trudi mounted smaller ponies and came behind us. Jacob was almost ridden down as Catherine started off for the gateway.

There was a yellow moon up over the eastern mountains shedding quite a fair light.

My horse started off with a bang as if trying to shoot ahead of everybody and throw me in their paths. He took some holding and my legs got the first rasping on his impatient sides.

I began to wish I knew more about it. My moor ponies began to seem like fireside cats in comparison with this great brute.

He came back to my checking, but he didn't like it. He didn't like me either and kept side stepping. He nearly got my leg between him and the gatepost, but I got him away with about a quarter inch to go.

Catherine rode on out. My brute started to go again and I had to check and check and he started his sideways jinking again.

'Jason!' Catherine snapped out.

Jason took no notice but made an effort to open out into a gallop and this time when I checked he reared up, possibly with a notion of rolling on his back with me underneath.

In the midst of the heated argument I caught glimpses of Catherine pulling up her steed and the following girls holding their ponies well clear. They knew Jason better than I did.

Then into my bemused brain came the old adage, 'if you can't beat 'em, join 'em'—at least, till they get the idea they're winning.

'Okay!' I shouted, eased the rein and slapped his neck.

'What ho!' I could almost hear the damned horse thinking out loud as he put himself to it and started off along the track like an accelerating locomotive.

It was terrifying. He was a great, big, overpowered hell horse with the speed of his master, the Devil. How he missed the trees on that narrow track I do not know, but we thundered on with me clinging halfway up his neck, a poor, beaten jockey.

And then suddenly we got together. It had a dramatic effect on Jason and on me, too. We got into the right gait, and some kind of understanding filled our opposite souls.

He eased down, he let me turn him and we cantered back, not subdued, but not so rebellious, to the others.

Catherine nodded. I turned the big horse and came beside her and we started off.

'I want to see the car,' she said.

'I'll show you.'

We rode the track and then turned in amongst the trees and down the slopes towards the car in the undergrowth. The thick carpet of pine needles made us strangely quiet, like phantom riders.

We came down to where I had left the rented Merc and I looked round. We rode a little farther, then turned and came back in a wider sweep. We stopped.

'Well?' she said, distrustfully.

'It seems to have been towed away,' I said. 'I must make out a claim form for my pyjamas.'

Catherine looked back to the girls behind us then turned to me.

'You have been telling the truth?' she said.

'Certainly. What purpose could I have in lying?'

'You left the car here?'

'It ran dry.'

'You were alone?'

I began to get the drift. She was getting it wrong.

'Of course I was alone. If you're beginning to think this is some dodge to get back into your

26

establishment and spy, you can forget it before you waste too much mental energy. Everything I told you is true.'

'Then where is the car?'

'I'll make sure the place is right,' I said, and got off and gave the rein to Trudi. Jason did not seem to mind. Perhaps he just didn't like men.

I went around the ground in the moonlight until I found the mush tracks of the tyres in the needles. Obviously the car had been pulled back up the same tracks, for there were no others. It was lucky there were any at all, for I became less and less sure that I was at the right place until I saw them.

'This is the place,' I said, pointing. 'You can just see tracks going back up to the lane—your lane.'

And then I saw two articles lying by the bushes—at least, one was lying, the other had fallen so as to get hooked on the brambles.

The one on the bush was an old car rug I use for covering over the luggage in the boot; the other a thin golfing type waterproof jacket that comes in handy in bad weather.

But the jacket was dark stained and wet. Even by moonlight I could see that it was blood.

The girls were watching me intently as I held the jacket lightly by its hanging loop and bent for the rug. I just knew there was going to be something wrong when I tugged it off the brambles.

Something fell from it and tumbled to the needled floor. It lay there like a small, crumpled ball of silver paper shining as it caught the moon coming down through the pines.

I picked it up.

'What is it?' Catherine commanded.

'A battered bullet,' I said. 'And there's blood on this jacket of mine. I'm sorry. It appears I didn't tell you the truth, after all.'

2

She dismounted and came silently to me.

'Explain yourself,' she said.

'It would seem they were not firing at me, those Porsche-men,' I said. 'There must have been someone hiding in my boot. Someone who got hit by one bullet. This one penetrated the boot but got smashed on the way and dropped into the rug.

'Possibly a third got my gas tank, which would account for the amazing coincidence of my running out at a crucial point in the pursuit.'

'Who did you hide there?' she said, narrow eyed.

'My dear Kate, this is nothing to do with me. I was the unconscious chauffeur.'

'How would this happen without your knowing?'

'I can only think somebody crawled in the boot while I feasted at the deserted

28

Schnitzelhaus. What else?'

'You explain too easily,' she said angrily. 'And why do you call me Kate? I am the Countess Catherine . . .' and out came the string of names and titles like a tape reciting a minor mitropan geography.

'It's friendly. I am always friendly when worried.'

'You're the biggest bloody fool I have ever come across!'

'I love your English and astuteness.'

'Why do you always joke?'

'It's something to do while I'm thinking. I'm thinking my passenger must have been alive. He wasn't dumped. He got in himself or was helped in, but he was still worth killing, you understand.'

'If you tell the truth,' she said angrily, 'then you were followed here.'

'It would seem like that. But the Porsche might have come back, having lost me, and taken a closer look. That would be a logical course of events.'

'How come these things are left here?'

'I picture the corpse being pulled out of the boot and these came out with him.'

'Why not just take the car with him inside?'

'They wanted to see what state he was in, dead or alive. They couldn't have known he was dead, could they?'

'You smile suddenly. Why?'

'Because suddenly I realised it lets me out.

29

They won't bother with me any more—'

'But you are a witness, they shot at you, damaged the car, stole it?'

'Yes. I was too happy too suddenly,' I admitted. 'I'm like that. If I get depressed I come up again like a ball. Then I hit the ceiling and come down again.'

'You are a manic depressive,' she said.

'I wouldn't know. I once had an interview with a psychiatrist and it proved he was mad.'

Her beautiful humourless face began to melt. Such simple stuff seemed to be the way to her heart. Simple humour. Banana skin wit.

But the softening was only a suggestion of a break in the piling clouds. It was a thought of what might be useful later, certainly not then.

I went back up the slope following the ruts, such as they were. They were intermittent, and just flattened hollows at that. Unless you knew something had been down there, the signs would have meant nothing.

On the main track there was no sign at all. My faithful followers were close behind, even Jason allowing himself to be led. Kate followed me looking more as if she would shoot me in the back than to learn anything.

'Well, there it is,' I said. 'They could only have gone away from your house. Perhaps we should go that way.'

Kate signalled to her guard and remounted her horse without help. She was a lithe beast. I don't think she had been waited on quite as much as I had thought at first.

Mounted again, Jason threw his head about a bit to show that all was not yet forgiven, but then went on quite easily.

We came to the road and halted there.

'Which way would you guess?' I asked.

She shrugged.

'If he was killed for *Them*—' she jerked her head to the East, '—then that way. If to keep him from Them, then this.'

'You think it could be either?'

'It is very difficult to tell, so close to the frontier as this.'

'What is it usually?'

'One does not hear—usually.' She was stiff then.

'But you know. It is an interest of yours, isn't it?'

Again a shrug.

'Why do you have a guard?' I asked. 'What are you afraid of?'

It was the wrong question. She blew up.

'I am afraid of nothing! Nothing!' She lashed out with her crop and hit me on the shoulder. It stung.

I edged Jason away.

'Then why have a guard?' I persisted.

'We go back,' she said abruptly.

'Oh, not yet,' I said. 'I can see the car.'

That stopped her. I rode ahead. Towards the road bend which curved round to the level crossing there was a thicket down a slope on the right. Some way down the slope of the embankment I could see a patch of white. I couldn't see that it was a car, but I felt it was worth taking a look at in the circumstances.

'Don't go!'

Her voice was commanding, so much so that, taken by surprise, I hauled back on Jason and he—also as if surprised—actually halted.

I looked back at her. She sat rigid as a statue for a moment, head cocked, listening. I could hear nothing but the restless sounds of the horses.

'It is a snare!' she said briefly, and rode past me to the point on the road above the car.

She didn't lack courage if she thought that. She stopped, looking down at the white patch, her hand upheld to stop us following.

It was interesting to conjecture why she had sensed a trap there. By all normal—or abnormal rules, as you wish—there was no sign of one. It seemed to me to point to a fact that she knew a lot more about such things than I had suspected.

In fact it showed she knew a damned sight more than I with all my turgid experience in the past. Or it could be she knew local signs, and I didn't.

She remained quite still, then dismounted.

'Not alone, you're not,' I said, and rode Jason up to her mount. She had just started down the slope then and looked quickly back. I followed her a pace or two behind. The girls

32

rode quietly up to our horses above us.

The further down we got the less we could see of the white patch in the thicket owing to our angle of sight flattening as we got near it.

Which made it seem that the car had fallen down from out of the sky rather than rolled down the slope into the undergrowth.

I got her by the arm then.

'Hold it,' I said quietly.

She held it. She kept dead still watching the white painted metal. Somewhere behind the undergrowth there was a slight sound. It could have been any creature, sneaking away, frightened by our approach.

But it didn't go far, for it stopped and there was quiet down there. Far off there came the double moo of air horns. Another train coming. Or possibly running into the frontier station.

Looking back a moment I saw that one girl held the loose horses. The other remained mounted, but her gun was in her hand pointing down over our heads at the car.

It was a small but comforting touch.

There were loose stones in patches on the slope where rains had washed away the earth. I bent down and got a good stone, then threw it into the thicket.

It crashed through the young trees and hit the metal with a clang that started some birds up from the midnight roost.

The rustle, squeaking and confusion was

momentary on the part of the natural inhabitants of that place.

But somebody groaned.

She started forward. I got her and pulled her back.

'Stay there. It's a trick. Remember?' I whispered it close to her ear and she stayed rigid, staring into the thicket.

The groaning was short and quiet and came again over the dark thicket.

A trick, of course. Who the hell would groan knowing there were guns covering his hideout? Only someone who knew he had more than guns to offer.

The train hooted again. It was a distraction. I almost felt it was deliberate.

I moved aside, going away from the bit of car that showed. I watched Kate from the corner of my eye to be sure she did not move. I felt that if anyone hid near the car wreck he wouldn't dare shoot at her while the girls above had her covered.

There was another groan, a muffled sound. This time it seemed like someone struggling for breath more than just a person who had been hurt.

And then came the idea that confused the whole issue.

There could well be someone hurt; the man in my boot who had been shot.

I went nearer the fringe of the little trees and looked sideways along to the car.

At first the sight was difficult to believe. There was no car there, just trees forever and ever on either side of where the car should have been.

I went back a few paces and looked again. The car was still there, gleaming white against the dark whips of the little trees.

No mistaking it. I could even see the silver badge from where I stood and part of the number plate.

But back into the edge of the wood I saw no car at all.

Just a thin, bent line, a hook, an angle.

When once you doubt your eyesight it is hard to make it see what is really there, as if the sight sulks because you won't believe it and refuses to see it again as before.

And then my eyes clicked on.

It was no car, but just the boot lid.

I went deeper into the little wood, going very quietly now that I was sure some kind of booby trap was indicated by the boot lid. I could not see such a lid being wrenched off, or thrown off in a crash, because its shape was as before.

It must have been deliberately taken off, and there must have been a reason for that.

I would have left it right there, the whole set-up, but for the idea that the groaner was a victim and not a siren.

Further, to get that man who had ridden with me unknown would be to solve the mystery. As I stood, suspected and friendless at

35

the far off edge of Nowhere, my position was unpleasant. One party, I knew, but who the others were I could not guess.

And either side had too many guns for my sense of fitness. When I had none at all.

The wood was dead quiet then. Up on the road I heard one of the horses toss his head restlessly, making his fitments jingle. He also blew a raspberry and I heard iron shoes scraping impatiently on the hard road.

I started to curve through the little tree clumps towards the boot lid.

Then suddenly one horse whinied as if terrified. It was an awful sound and stopped me dead in my tracks.

I heard a gunshot from above, and then another. Something moved ahead of me and I threw myself face down to the ground, not realising it was a sliver of tree ripped by a bullet.

But it was a good thing, anyhow.

There was a blaze of flame such as I have never seen close. It flashed through the little trees in a brilliant flash of orange lightning.

The ground shook. Little trees started to rain on me, bits of branches, twigs, earth, stones, and the air blasting past me was searing hot.

The booby trap had gone off.

CHAPTER THREE

1

For almost a minute after the explosion it seemed the wood was on fire. The fierce blast of fiery air rushed over me and to my strained nerves the explosion sounded more like a prolonged roaring, as from a continuous series of explosions.

Gradually the ferocity died away and there was nothing but a smouldering smell in the still air. I got up then, gingerly. Against the yellow sky the boot lid of my hired car could be seen, twisted and blackened, stuck up near the top of a tree. The general vegetation seemed to have suffered less than I would have expected from the blast.

I looked aside up the slope to the road, the two girls were rising up from where they had ducked the fire storm. Catherine was in the act of getting to her feet, half way up the slope.

There was no further movement inside the wood. The groans of the unseen sufferer had stopped.

At that time I was sure that some kind of booby trap had been planted near the boot lid, but that one of the girl's shots from the road above had set it off. It was lucky they had fired, for without that sudden sight of a sapling bullet-splitting ahead of me I wouldn't have flattened myself as I did.

But what had the girls seen to make them shoot?

The idea of going back up to ask them seemed a long way round when I was down in the wood already. So I went on towards the scene of the explosion.

There was a hole and a circle of blackened vegetation around it. It had blown the middle of a narrow path through the tangled little trees, a path one would naturally have followed if one had gone straight in for the boot lid.

Keeping well to one side I went on along the path. It snaked along, a bend every yard almost, so that I did not see the fallen man until I was almost on him. He sprawled face down on the ground, one leg bent, hands clawing ahead of him, as if he had been trying to crawl away when the blast got him from behind.

I took a good look round me, peering into the silent wood, before I knelt down to take a closer look at him.

He had a bullet wound in one shoulder which had not been attended to and a lot of blood soaked his shirt. The fact it was still bleeding slightly showed he wasn't yet dead, though he looked very close to it then.

I turned quickly as I heard a twig snap. Catherine came into view, her pistol held at the ready, Trudi behind her, similarly equipped.

They both stopped. Kate watched the man on the ground, Trudi watched me. She didn't trust me.

38

'Know him?' I asked Kate.

She kept on looking down. I had the idea that she was trying to make up her mind what to reply to my question.

'Yes,' she said at last. 'We must get him back.'

'We need a hurdle or something suitable.'

Kate nodded to Trudi, who turned, with a distrustful glance at me and went away back down the path.

'Who is he?'

'It is Franz Reiz.'

'Is he mixed up in political matters? Spying?'

She did not answer but stayed looking down at him as if he meant more to her than showed before.

'Is the wound serious?' she asked.

'No. But he's lost blood. I think the blast finished off what strength he had.' I looked around the shadowy wood again, thinking I heard something move.

'It is the train,' she said.

The sound grew and soon I recognised it, running on the air now instead of the ground. The air horns hooted mournfully, warning the crossing where I had so nearly bought it.

'Why should he hide in my boot?' I asked.

She shrugged and did not answer.

'To get here?' I went on. 'But how did he know I would come here?'

'He took a risk, I suppose,' she said angrily. 'You were heading this way, were you not?'

39

'If he got in at the Schnitzelhaus,' I said, 'how was it the followers took forty miles to catch up? Or was it deliberately done on your doorstep?'

'Of course it was! They are my enemies!'

'Up to now you've held out that you couldn't guess who they were,' I said. 'Does this mean the identity of this man gave you the information?'

'This man has one meaning for me,' she said, bitterly. 'That all I have fought to prevent has happened. I might as well have done nothing at all. Everything we have done is a waste. A terrible, awful waste!'

For the first time she showed signs that she was a woman with normal, human feelings. She was shaken, hurt, very distressed.

She knelt by the man and began to rip the shirt. Her playing the hard act had completely finished.

'Leave him till we get him back,' I said. 'There's nothing you can do here without water or anything else. He's bled enough. It's almost stopped. We should get him to a hospital for a transfusion.'

'No!' She became rigid, horrified at the idea. 'No! We must do it ourselves.'

'You can't leave him without an injection of blood,' I said. 'He's got to have that, no matter what you say.'

'Maurer,' she said suddenly. 'We shall fetch him. He can be trusted to a point.'

40

'What point?' I said, watching her closely. 'Gun point?'

'He will do it for money,' she said, contemptuously. 'He will do anything for that.'

The two girls came back with a gate. It was very light. I wondered if it would carry Reiz, for he was not specially small.

We got him on it and I took the front with the two girls taking a corner each at the back. The gate bent like a bow under the weight. We started through the wood, back past the burnt area of the bomb, edging past the trees with the gate which at times was almost wider than the pathway.

As we went I kept a good eye open, but nothing appeared that could be construed as a danger to us.

I had time to think a little of what I had run into. Machine gun firing from car to car on a highway; bombs in a wood. It looked like a no-holds-barred society. Not my kind at all.

We got him up to the road.

'Put him across my saddle,' Kate said.

I humped him over, face down, like a sack of spuds. She mounted behind him and started off back down the track to the hunting lodge. I followed with the two girls.

The night was still, our hoofbeats echoed in the pines and the moon, gathering strength through the thinning clouds, threw our black shadows on the track.

We came back into the stabling yard. Jacob

41

came out to attend the horses, but looked to me rather drunk.

They seemed to have everything handy, even a stretcher which the girls fetched. The four of them together took Reiz away to a room quite near the back entrance to the lodge.

I went on through into the hall again, Trudi following me having deposited the victim with her companions.

'We go for Maurer, you and I,' she said, her hand on the belt of her jeans where her gun was.

'On a horse?' I said.

'We take a car. I will show you.'

Her English did not seem anywhere as good as Kate's. Sometimes it came easily and sometimes it jammed up.

We went out and through another corridor into a yard. Over the wall we could hear the horses snorting and Jacob cursing. There were two cars in the yard. She went to an Impala and got in the passenger seat. She just sat there, her head cocked looking at me.

I got in and started up. She reached forward and pressed a button. The top rolled back over our heads and folded away at the rear.

'Isn't that unwise?' I said.

'There is very little intelligence in keeping hidden what is already known,' she said.

'Except that it makes us easier to shoot at.'

'That will not happen yet,' she said. 'Go ahead over the train crossing to the highway

42

and turn to the right.'

'We head for the frontier town?'

She nodded. I trod and we slipped out of the yard and back along the track down to the road. It was smoother, better, easier to handle than Jason.

'What is that man to Catherine?' I said as we curved round to the crossing.

'He was a servant to her brother. It means that her brother is taken. That much is what it means.'

'Taken where? By whom?'

'Across the frontier. By Them. You understand. It happens often.'

'It's a regular traffic? I mean a lot of people vanish across the border?'

'Some. One can never tell when it happens.'

We crossed the tracks and got on to the highway, continuing an interrupted journey.

There was heavy stuff going both ways, one or two cars threading in amongst them. It was a third-rate highway.

Then through the trees we saw lights coming up against the purple of distant mountains.

'You take to the right,' she said. 'The first.'

We took to the right the first. It came round amongst a lot of wooden buildings with eaves like fir trees and parked on either side of wide places, more like a wild west layout than a Western street.

'You go over there, and stop by the steps.'

I went over to one of the wooden houses and

stopped by some steps that went up to a first floor. Judging by the carved signs on the ground floor it belonged to a toymaker, wheelmaker, cabinet maker or somebody good at the wood.

We got out and went up the steps. They turned into a porch so that none from the street could see who called. Trudi shoved the bell in a kind of code. Nothing happened.

'Nobody in,' I said.

'He will come,' she replied, and then raising her short riding boot she kicked the door so that I thought the panels would split and let us in that way.

The door opened suddenly. She just walked in and the man behind the door retreated.

I followed her in. The man stood back then, or rather staggered back. He seemed rich in booze, judging from his poor balance and by the smell he would have failed a B-test at ten feet.

He shouted something in German or Russian. It could have been anything, and the girl turned and spat something out at him that rocked him back as if she had hit him.

'This man comes,' she said, pointing to me.

He turned to me. The first sight of him was rather like meeting a bear who has made a poor attempt to shave. He had hair all round a pair of gold spectacles, narrow as slots, over which he peered with large, bulging bloodshot eyes. He wore a sagging collection of velvet clothes

44

and a fancy silk shirt shot with drink of many colours.

'I can do no more!' he shouted at me. 'I can do no more for nobody. They will suspect. To hell with it and crumpets.'

'Crumpets!' I said.

'I have crumpets in England,' he said, and to express his opinion of them imitated a belch that rocked the room. 'I can do nothing for you—'

'The Countess of—' I reeled off as many titles as I could remember, '—wants you at once with blood plasma.'

True to his reputation he made no reply but cocked his head and rubbed his thumb and forefinger together, indicating money.

'When you have done, you snuffling pig,' Trudi said. 'Get your things. We go!'

Maurer shrugged, then looked at me and stroked his jaw.

'Here,' he said, 'I speak with you as I get these things.'

'Okay,' I said, and looked at the girl.

She just nodded. She was beginning to trust me.

2

Mauer took me into his surgery. I call it that for want of something better to describe a heaped-up layout of medicines, drugs, booze, dressings, instruments, scales, littered couches, tables, books, magazines, coffee pots and dirty cups,

45

cigarette ends, the lot. Pleasure, work, vice, hope, occupation and amusement all mixed up in a big, dirty heap.

'I keep blood in the fridge,' he said, and shoved past an overloaded table to a domestic fridge in a corner. Magazines and a stethoscope fell to the floor as he went.

'Do you have patients?' I said, staring round.

'Good ones,' he said. 'There is quite good commerce in patients who wish no fuss these days. I used to alter people's faces. Cut Jewish noses down to size. That was a while back.'

I looked at the window. It was hard to think of people being treated for anything in the middle of this filth.

He took out jars and started filling up an ancient leather bag of 1890 type. He tossed in instruments, dressings, antiseptics just as he snatched them up from the littered tables and shelves.

'Ready,' he said, and then put the bag back on a table. 'Why do you come in this? Who are you, Englander?'

'I'm a tourist. Nothing special.'

I saw Trudi standing by the open doorway in the passage, but Maurer did not see her.

'Drink with me,' he said, bringing a bottle off a shelf.

'We must go,' I said.

'What wound is this?'

'I told you. A shoulder.'

He shrugged expressively and brought two

46

misty looking glasses off another shelf.

'It takes many days for gangrene to set in,' he said.

'Look, the man is wounded. Very short of blood. He needs you now.'

'But supposing there is nobody to attend him? There is only one me. I do not go yet. He will live. If he dies, then there must be something wrong with him anyhow. Drink with me. Wish me luck.'

'I think it's the patient who needs it,' I said.

He poured vodka generously into two glasses.

'If you do not drink with me, then I do not go. I am superstitious. Life is dangerous for me. I need to have something to believe in. Drink.'

'Then you come,' I said, taking up a glass.

'Oh, then I come, of course,' he said, swinging his glass in the air. 'But I am the artist, you understand. I have to feel right, have the right moment. Prost.'

'Prost.'

I swallowed mine without looking too closely at the glass.

'Another,' he said, holding out a dirty hand.

It was like Kate's game of toasts.

'No,' I said. 'You come on. The man may be dying.'

'Ah, that is very sad,' he said, refilling the glasses. 'Man never knows how close he may be to the grand moment. Prost.'

Trudi was standing quite at ease, watching

us. I did not see what I could do. We had to have a black market doctor, and this was the only one available. The possibility was that if he was not pleased, he would not come at all.

So I drank.

'Now come on,' I said.

'No, no,' he said. 'Two is for sorrow. Three is better for all good luck. Three is the correct number.' His hand was steady as he poured out more vodka, though before the first drink it had been definitely shaky.

The thought occurred that perhaps he had to stoke up to steady himself before he could do anything delicate. Dedicated boozers often come like that.

At about that time I saw Trudi was smiling, as if amused.

'Now come on,' I said. 'Otherwise there'll be no money.'

'Money is not everything. You insult me,' he said, pouring again. 'My vocation is sacred, my skill of priceless worth. That is the only reason I charge money for what I do. Because it is so priceless that whatever I charge it is too little. So that—prost.'

'I don't want any more.'

'Then I do not come. I go nowhere with tee-totallers. I am degraded with such and do not allow it.' He drank more so thirstily it looked as if he had not drunk for days.

'Look, Doctor, the man is ill. Come now or there will be no pay.'

'You insult me, by God! I shall not come. You will go alone. Tell her I am insulted and refuse!'

Trudi was still quite calm, as if she were quite used to this behaviour. Or perhaps it was because she would sooner have Reiz dead than alive. Either way, I found myself up against two of them. I had no idea of what to do to make the man move. I just didn't know the rules of this game.

Then Trudi took it over.

She pulled her pistol from her belt and levelled it at Maurer's glass. She took aim very slowly as he raised the glass to give a toast before swallowing it like the others.

She fired and the glass shattered out of his fingers, just the thick bottom falling to the filthy carpet and rolling away.

'Okay, okay!' he shouted, grabbing up a hat from under a lot of periodicals. 'I come!'

He took up his bag and came out with us like a child. It seemed Trudi knew just how far to let him go before she could break him down.

We went out and into the porch preparatory to going down the steps to the car. Maurer started to go down then turned about and came up again, banging into me. He shoved past and got to the porch just as I caught his sleeve.

'What's the game?' I said.

'The man down there,' he said and went on.

I followed him. Trudi having been ahead and shown herself to whoever it was down there,

49

carried on to the car.

'Who is he?' I said.

'A man best not to meet,' Maurer said. 'For me. Maybe for you, too. I would not advise the fool-hardy.'

'The girl has gone down,' I said.

'She does not know him,' Maurer said.

He looked shaken, even frightened. I left him there and went down a short way until I could see round the angle of the building. A man stood by the side of the Impala watching the girl get in. She took no notice of him at all in proper Continental style. He stared at her as if to go right through, also Continental style.

She settled herself. He raised his face a moment to look up.

Maurer's face had been dirty, shaggy, but bearlike and therefore not repulsive. But the face of the man down there was repulsive, ugly and evil to an extent I had never seen before.

He seemed to glow with it, like a Chinese torturer watching his victim's bowels slowly being pulled out. He was dark, thick with a mouth a foot wide, thick lipped, a black beard underchin, no moustache but to make up his thick brows joined in the middle. He stood about six feet two and four across. He was the nearest thing in shape to a well-groomed ape that I had ever seen.

'What's his name?' I said.

'Mort,' said Maurer.

'Bloody good name for a French maniac,' I

50

said.

'You know him?' the drunken doctor said quickly.

'No.'

'He is from Marseilles. He breaks men to little bits. It is an amusement. But he has a big job.'

'What is it?'

'He runs a transfer agency. He sells them across the border if they want the merchandise, he sells them. No matter where they are hiding, he will get them and bring them across. He is very rich.'

'Why should he be interested in us?'

'His interests are wide.'

'You mean he's after you. That's why you won't go down.'

'I do not court death. It is a tiresome process. I see much of it.'

Mort stood near the car still, staring at the girl. She seemed perfectly composed, looking straight ahead of her.

I rejoined Maurer in the porch.

'Is that man following us to find out where you're being called to?'

'I should imagine. Yes, it would be that.'

'Does he do this often?'

'He has done it before. He never loses a chance of new commerce.'

'Is it just unfortunate that he has picked tonight?'

'What else?'

'Can he watch your premises from his office?'

'No.'

'Then he must have come especially. It is getting very late. He wouldn't have been waiting on the off-chance.'

'But how did he know you would come?'

I thought of the car gunmen and the booby trap in the woods and it seemed that it was not too difficult to guess how Mort had got some inkling of the night's affairs.

Specially if the car men and bomb layers had been his own characters, or travel agents, you might say.

But there was a weakness. If Mort was the big man in this town, as Maurer hinted, then he would have had no need to have shot up my car, planted bombs or do anything else but wait in the town for me to drive in.

With that it began to look as if we might be in between two gangs. Mort versus The Rest; for versus read me.

'He seems to have nobody with him,' I said after watching the street for a few seconds.

'He is content just with himself. He is very powerful.'

Mort seemed quite unconscious of being watched. He just stared at the girl all the time.

In height we were not far short of a match, but in weight, width, reach, we were far from it. The only thing was that I practised judo in a sporting club I belong to. Judo makes a truism

52

of the remark that the bigger they are the harder they fall.

Always providing that the other chap doesn't know it as well.

'Does he know whose car that is?' I said.

'Yes. He will know that. That is why he is there. He puts the screw on Catherine because of her brother.'

'Why?' My interest grew very sharp.

'He is wanted the other side, the brother. Mort is taking both payments right now, judging which will finally be the highest.'

I thought I could see the framework of the whole thing. Reiz, left wounded and unimportant, had been the brother's companion. Reiz being left like that meant just that the brother was no longer in need of a bodyguard. As Trudi had guessed.

That was why Catherine had been so upset.

An idea occurred to me because (a) I liked Catherine and (b) I took an instant dislike to Mort.

'Get a hypo ready,' I said. 'I want a knock-out drop ready to push in.'

'You mean that? What is wrong?'

'Get it ready.'

My tone convinced him he had better for he put his bag on a wooden seat in the porch and opened up. In a moment he had a needle shoved into the rubber cap of some colourless liquid which I hoped wasn't more vodka.

'Wait till I give you the signal,' I said, and

went down the stairs to the street.

Neither Trudi nor Mort looked towards me as I came down and rounded the car so as to get into the driver's seat.

Mort looked at me then, and he was certainly big. The nearer one got to him the bigger he got. He did not move. Which was a pity.

Until he did move my art wasn't any good against a man so large. Overcoming his inertia would be a hefty job and use up energy that might be needed later.

Just when I thought he would not move at all, he put out a hand to shove into my chest.

Nothing could have been nicer. I got him, twisted and slung him back against the side of the door so that his big head rocked on his thick neck.

He came back as a fighter bouncing from the ropes, swiping out with a leg of mutton fist. I caught it and threw it over my shoulder as I turned and he went in a somersault and landed flat on his back on the dusty road.

He rolled over and was up again, crouching now, more apelike than ever but grinning as if he had now got my measure.

He started moving about like a wrestler trying to lead me into a bad position. I didn't move at all, just watched him. Sometimes you can see better if you don't move.

He started weaving round and I turned to keep facing him. He got his back against the

54

stairs to Maurer's flat. The doctor started to creep down, with his needle ready.

That was the moment when, sensing danger, Mort turned his head and saw the doctor.

And that was when he laughed.

CHAPTER FOUR

1

Mort backed sideways along the wall of the woodworker's shop, so as to keep both Maurer and me in sight. The girl sat in the car watching.

Mort was such a huge man that I thought he was easily within catching distance. But he moved much quicker than I had thought possible for such a bulk.

He stepped back another pace which brought him level with the workshop door, and then he reached out, got the handle, slapped the door open and stepped inside, all in a split second.

When I ran forward the door was already shut.

It was not locked, however. I looked back to the girl.

'Your gun,' I said, holding out my hand.

'No,' she said, as simply as that.

So I opened the door and went in, stepping smartly to one side as soon as within, so I didn't show up against the moonlight from without.

It was quiet in there but an irritating wooden ticking like crickets made it hard to hear very small sounds. There were half a dozen toy wooden clocks ticking away.

The scene inside that place was like some pantomime nightmare. Great carved faces, grotesque horses' heads, bulls' masks, totem poles, all crowded around and staring at me with great glaring eyeballs and teeth like phosphorescent tombstones.

Not only were they terrifying to view, but jumbled and piled about anywhere as they were, they hid Mort.

Clearly he knew his way about here, so that he had every advantage, including the fact that he knew I meant to be unfriendly.

I did not think that he had a gun or he would have used it earlier, but in such a cluttered place as this, with him knowing the route and me not, it was just foolish to stay.

As I backed very quietly to the door I heard a voice. With the confused ticking of the wooden clocks and the general damping effect of the massed wooden figures I couldn't tell where the speaker was.

But the single word he said riveted my feet to the floor and gave me a shivering feeling at the back of my neck.

'Blake!' Mort said.

Now what I had told Kate was true. Austria was a new country to me. I had never been there, could have known nobody, and had no business, introductions or involvements.

Yet the stranger spoke my name without hesitation.

Taken aback by the sound of my own name, I just stood there and he spoke it again, louder. He could see I had not gone out again through the moonlit door, and I guessed he knew there was no other way except by passing him, wherever he was.

There seemed little point in denying my name.

'What?' I said.

'You should speak with me, not fight.'

'Okay. Speak what you have to say. But I am in a hurry.'

'Bon. You hurry now, but you see me tomorrow. At four. Bundestrasse 22.'

'This is a strange situation for an invitation to tea.'

'I have something that you will want. Do not neglect the opportunity. Go now.'

I backed out, very watchfully, but there was no sign of movement in pursuit. When I got in the car the shop door stayed yawning blackly, and nobody came out.

'You have lost him?' Trudi said, with a faint smile.

'I don't think so,' I said. 'Where's Maurer?'

'Behind,' she said.

I looked over the back of the front seats and there he was crouching on the floor, trying to hide his whole body under his battered

Homburg, so it looked.

We started off, swung round and hared back the way we had come. The night was still. Even on the highway the mastodon trains, like elephants holding each other's tails, were mostly parked in the laybys.

We came into the yard behind the hunting lodge at one-fifteen. A couple of the girls were waiting. They took Maurer, one at each elbow, and shoved him into the house clutching his old bag to his chest. His hat fell off and rolled on the cobbles at my feet. I picked it up and followed them into the house with Trudi behind me. She liked to be behind me. She was a watchful character.

When we came into the great hall Kate was pouring coffee and smoking a cigarette.

'You are just in time,' she said coldly.

'There was an interruption and Maurer didn't want to come.'

'What interruption?' she said, looking up sharply.

I told her about Mort. She stayed very still, looking past me at the wall.

'How did he know you?' she said, looking back to me with narrowed eyes.

'That's my problem,' I said. 'In fact, I thought it must be that you had telephoned him, told him we were coming and for him to sort of guard the proceedings. I couldn't think how else he could know my name.'

'I telephoned nobody,' she said, and began

58

to walk slowly away alongside the huge refectory table. 'So it would seem that the story you told me to begin with was lies.'

She stopped and turned quickly. She looked very angry then.

From the corner of my eye I saw Trudi's hand go to the pistol in her belt. At almost the same time the two girls who had taken Maurer to the wounded man came back into the hall through another door. They stopped, watching the scene.

There was a moment of very unpleasant silence.

'I told you the truth,' I said.

She laughed contemptuously.

'You are a liar. You are concerned with this and our enemies know you. That is the truth, is it not?'

'No. I know no one here except you. Is Mort an enemy?'

'He's everyone's enemy. Everyone's spy. Everyone's murderer. It should be interesting when you go to him—for tea!'

'I don't propose to go. This Merry Widow set-up is of no interest to me. If I've done what I can for you, I'll get back on the highway and thumb a lift.'

'Where to?'

'That way,' I said pointing. 'Away from you and that big stinker at Bundestrasse 22. I just want to go home.'

She sat down in one of the empty chairs,

leant an elbow and rested her chin on her hand. She was very beautiful. Even without candlelight she would have been beautiful.

She sat there, watching me. I lit a cigarette, took a chair out from its place and sat down.

'You're a liar but very poor,' Kate said. 'You would not go. You have some interest here. What is it?'

'I have none!'

'Which side do you play?'

'I'm on your side, whatever that is.'

She laughed again, and it was not nice.

'But,' I went on, 'I'd sooner be on no side and go home. I would walk out, but I think Trudi would shoot me. She is a cold pudding.'

I saw Trudi's ice-blue eyes sharpen up and her full lips twisted just a little.

'Why do you think she would shoot?' Kate said.

'I just have the feeling. An instinct. She would do it for fun. She is a happy girl in a quiet way.' I leant on the table. 'Why don't you tell me what this is all about, or do I know? Is it your brother?'

She watched me for a while.

'Yes,' she said at last. 'He has been taken.'

'Is this a political business, or personal?'

'It is personal, but covered by politics. If one uses politics one can bring in such large forces to your side. That is, if you are on the far side of the frontier. On this side we are not so fortunate.'

60

'What do you mean to do? Get him out again?'
Her face hardened.
'Of course!'
'Just you and—and four girls?' I said incredulously.
'Of course.'
'Up against that lot!' I said. 'You must be joking!'
She started up then.
'I do not joke! It is my brother who is there. I shall get him out of their hands no matter what the price.'
'Just a minute!' I got firm then and she reacted quite smartly, stopping in the act of walking away. 'What has your brother supposed to have done?'
She frowned at me, searching my eyes.
'A frame-up, you call it,' she said. 'But they think that he was instrumental in having a man captured in Vienna. One of their agents.'
'Who was?'
'The son of a big man over the border. A chief of the State Police, Zdunek.'
'What happened to Zdunek junior?'
'He was shot. It was some kind of international mix-up. No one knows who fired the shot, but my brother is paying for it.'
'Where is your brother? Do you know that?'
'He is a prisoner in a *schloss* just five kilometres over the frontier. It is used as a holiday place for top party officials, also for political

61

prisoners.'

'It's a trap,' I said. 'They want you as well.'

'You think we have not thought of that?'

'Not hard enough, I would say. Not if you propose to go there.'

'We can do nothing from here.'

'If you go, they will be waiting for you.'

'They have waited some days yet. They will not know when we shall come.'

'Granted the advantage is with the attacker, you aren't strong enough. Besides which, it never does for girls to be taken.'

'They have as much courage as men.'

'That isn't quite the point. Let me see this. You mean to go in on your own one night, slip across, get to the castle, storm it, come away back over the frontier with all hell in pursuit.'

'We shall do it very quietly. We are well trained.'

'You don't know one small thing about the defence arrangements at the castle. You don't know the time the guards go round, do you? Or when they pull up the drawbridge or whatever it is.'

She shrugged.

'The man in there will know,' she said, pointing. 'When he is conscious again, he will tell.'

'It would be better,' I said, stamping out my cigarette, 'to engage the help of a professional scene shifter. My friend at Bundestrasse 22.'

'You would not trust such a man!'

'Look, he's in the business, Kate. This is the important angle. He makes money from his shifting people around. To do that kind of work you have to make sure what's at the other end to receive them.

'You say this castle is used as a politicians' holiday camp. That gives an excuse for a visitor. Assuming that Mort's business is an iceberg, with an eighth showing honestly above the surface, he knows the regular open ways to fix things on either side.

'He also knows which man to go to when over there, and who that man is likely to trust. Put it like this: he is the knowledgeable one. He is the man who sees both sides of the fence, where you see only the fence.'

'You do not know this man!'

'Do you?'

'No. But they are no good. None of that kind. Double dealers. Double crossers.'

'But I can deal that sort of game,' I said. 'I have had some experience. Sit down again. Let me tell you . . . .'

She looked at me and then, very slowly, sat down.

2

When we'd finished she still didn't trust me. But by then I had got so keen about it that I was rarin' to go. Enthusiasm sometimes persuades me I have won without any opposition. I am what is known as a hot-headed clunk.

All the same I had the feeling that I was right about Mort. He knew both sides of the fence, but also over the top and under the bottom. That's what men like Mort are for.

Money.

While we were talking, Maurer came in.

'He will be out six hours,' he said. 'But he will come to. I was just in time.'

He was just in time! He was, the sliding soak of Carinthia. It even puzzled me, the brazen face he put on it just for the sake of a rapid payout.

'There is a bed in his room,' Kate said. 'Sleep on it.'

'I am very thirsty, hard work has done me. Struggling, life and death—'

'Give him a bottle of wine,' Kate said, waving a hand at the two girls by the other door. 'And get rid of him!'

'After this rush to save life, this mad—' Maurer didn't have time to finish.

'Get out!' Kate said.

The two girls got him by his arms and frogged him out to the back of the house.

'It is late. We can do nothing more tonight,' Kate said. 'Guard him, Trudi. Room thirteen. I hope it will not be unlucky.'

It wasn't. Trudi wasn't a cold pudding, as it turned out. In fact, a hot one. She must have been the only guard I never wanted to get away from.

In the morning Reiz was critically ill. I

wondered if he had got some infection from Maurer's dirty equipment but was assured that it was fever due to such a loss of blood, shock and other matters.

Maurer assured me, personally.

He kept watch in a small room fitted with a table, chairs and a couple of beds. It seemed his bag contained several bottles of vodka, so his vigil was eased.

Once the day was with us Trudi became the stern guard once more, and to look at her one would hardly have guessed—

Or perhaps I would.

Kate didn't show up that morning. With the red-head Eva, and Trudi, we went riding to look again at the spot where the bomb had gone off in the wood.

One thing struck me then which in the pressure of events at night I hadn't thought important.

Somewhere the Mercedes was about with no boot lid, which must be unusual.

'It couldn't have got far,' I told the girls. 'It had no number. The cops would have got it.'

They did not seem impressed.

'Remember, too, that it had bullet holes in it,' I said. 'Surely that isn't so common round here?'

'It is not uncommon,' said Eva, 'for any cars that have something strange to be lost very quickly. Near the frontier like this, you find many dumped.'

'How far to the village you say is on the frontier?' I said.

'Two kilometres.'

'Let's go there,' I said. 'You never know. It would not be sensible to dump a car near a chap you believe you've murdered.'

'You have very peculiar logic,' said Trudi and shrugged.

We got going at a cracking pace, Jason doing his best to outdo the lot and me also. We left the road and went down through paths in the forest—for there was nothing small or thicketty about the trees here—and suddenly got a glimpse of what looked like a sugar cake village, glittering in the sunlight.

The garagier was a blacksmith who seemed to mend cracked-up looking vehicles with his bare fists and a hammer, judging by the look of the assortment that heaped up around his forge.

He looked at our horses with a questioning eye, thinking perhaps we wanted a shoe fixed.

Trudi asked the question. He shook his head, said a good deal, spat and wiped his mouth with the back of his hairy arm. He was practically all black with dirt.

I got down and slipped him a bar or so. He took up a thoughtful attitude. I slipped him another bar. The sum of the mazuma must have come to more than he had had or expected from the others.

He pocketed the notes, turned and ambled

away down the side of the forge to a yard which looked more like an orchard with rusted steel roots sprouting all around the trees.

Crammed up close to the back wall of the building was my rented car sans bootlid. He leant on the bonnet and regarded me as if he had made some remarkable personal achievement.

I pointed to the boot.

'The bags,' I said, then put it into German.

He shrugged and said a lot. I did not know whether it was a denial that any bags had been in it or whether it might be bought back for more money.

It turned out that he denied any bags had been in the car.

Which was a clear indication of how Mort had known my name. Probably everyone concerned with this undercover personnel shift knew it by now. Also the names of my tailor, shirtmaker, bank, and everyone else who had added their personal help to my trip.

I tried to think whether there had been anything in the cases which could have been of exceptional interest to local searchers but couldn't.

The blacksmith managed a sentence.

'You want the auto to take?'

'No,' I said slowly. 'But you'd better get a boot lid put on.'

He reached out to a lean-to shed by his side and pulled out a big sheet of steel, flicking it with his thumbnail. Then he nodded and held up two fingers.

'Two days,' he said, shoving the fingers almost in my face.

'Ja,' I said.

I had a look round inside the car while I was there but a few things which I had left lying around in it were still there. They were of no importance.

I switched on and the gas gauge showed some interest. So they had driven it here, not towed it.

And then I thought of the petrol tank. I indicated the back being lifted. He went off and came back pulling a jack. In a couple of seconds he had the back of the car high up and I looked underneath.

There were no bullet holes in the tank. But there was something about it that caught the eye.

The underside of the tank was grey with dried mud. But the drain plug edges were bright brass where a spanner had recently gripped it.

So it was not an accident that I had got no farther than I had. Design. Perhaps I had gone a little too far. Perhaps I was supposed to be stopped by the roadside when the sharp shooters arrived. True, they wouldn't have missed me then.

Which seemed to mean they had meant to come up the side road over the rail crossing and to get to this village.

As he lowered the car again, Trudi came up.

'Do you know my friends who brought this?' I said.

He scratched his dirty head and Trudi put it into a spitting sort of German. He drew himself up and I thought he was going to salute her.

He answered with a long guttural flow of language which missed me.

'It was only one man,' Trudi translated. 'He has described him but does not know him.'

'Where did the man go?' I said.

'He does not know. Come. We must go back.'

We left the blackened garagier, remounted and rode away. In the forest we dropped into a slow pace.

'Why did he accept me as the owner of the car when someone else brought it in?' I said. 'He must have known the man to know he wasn't the owner.'

'But why accept you?' Eva said. 'He knows you even less!'

'He knew the man,' Trudi said. 'I think he recognised him but cannot place him. Thus he not know if genuine. One often knows men to think, and then one is not sure. Some men are alike.'

'Did you recognise the description?'

My suspicions now switched to Trudi. She was a long time answering.

'It is like Catherine's brother,' she said at

last. 'But that could not be so, could it?'

'When was he taken?'

'Forty-eight hours. He could not be free like that.'

'Just a minute. Reiz escaped when the brother was taken?'

'That is what one heard.'

'What else did one hear? Was the brother rushed to the frontier regardless of Reiz being left behind?'

'I think he was, but that Reiz was chased and kept getting away, but he couldn't lose his pursuers.'

'It wouldn't be hard for them to hang on if they guessed he would come this way,' I said. 'Which sounds as if Reiz is far from being experienced at this sort of thing. The experienced don't fly straight to where the opposition think they will go.'

'Neither he nor Rudolph have anything to do with such things. Rudolph was in Vienna on business.'

'Wouldn't that smith have known Rudolph?' I said.

'He need not. No, I think he would not.'

'But this lodge is part of the old family estates?'

'Yes, but they keep to old tradition. They do not mix outside when they are here. And Rudolph comes rarely. The lodge is Catherine's.'

'Strange that such an aristocrat should be in

70

business,' I said. 'What business is it?'

'It is a very large store, with motor department and antiques of all kinds, with jewellery and valuable things.'

'In Vienna?'

'Indeed.'

'And he travels widely buying these antiques and the jewellery?'

'Of course he must.'

'Are you aware that this kind of business is widely used for the passing of international information, secret stuff?'

'Not Rudolph,' she said firmly.

'But cars as well,' I said. 'It is an odd combination.'

'He is as you say mad with them. He thinks more of the cars than of the priceless things.'

'Do you like him?'

The question shook Trudi. Eva, riding on my right hand, suddenly laughed and Trudi looked very angry for a moment before her usual icy look of calm came over again.

'I do not like him,' she said.

'Why not?'

'I do not like him.'

'Dr Fell,' I said.

'What?'

'Never mind. An idiom. Or could your dislike be for the fact that you do not trust him?'

'It is because he loves another woman,' Eva said. 'It is no good to hide, Trudi. You know that.'

It was odd that Trudi, who could throw her favours around as I knew she did, could be jealous of Rudolph, but there you are. That's often how it works out.

We quickened up then. It was an exhilarating ride through the forest and I hoped it might blow some of the confusion from my mind. It didn't.

I couldn't place the idea of dumping the car at a garage leaving a passable trail to the dumper. It would have been much easier to have junked it in the forest somewhere and walked away.

Only one sort of person might have chosen the way it had been done. A man dead mad about cars.

A man dead mad about cars who resembled Rudolph.

The idea of a double twist came into my mind then. Supposing Rudolph had not been taken at all? Supposing he was not the suffering ally, but aligned with the enemy?

And supposing the idea was not to get Rudolph, but to get Kate?

'I want to talk!' I shouted, pulling Jason up.

The others pulled up and turned back to me. I put my idea.

Eva laughed. Trudi thought about it, then shook her head.

'I cannot see that,' she said. 'For what purpose?'

72

'Perhaps the Vienna business isn't doing well,' I said. 'One never knows these things.'

'Impossible,' said Eva. 'We get back. It is late.'

So we rode back and came to the stable yard. Nobody came out to us. We tied the horses and went to look for Jacob.

The place was silent. We rang bells, shouted, and nothing happened. In the hall, we stood still a minute and shouted some more.

Nothing.

'Something has happened,' Trudi said, looking at me. 'Something like you said!'

CHAPTER FIVE

1

'Search everywhere,' Trudi said.

'Just a minute,' I said. 'Just in case there has been some kind of invasion here, we'd better keep together. You never know who's still around.'

'He is sensible,' Eva said. 'Do what he says.'

'You show me,' I said to Trudi.

So we went through the sumptuous house from room to room and down to the kitchens and didn't find a living soul. One or two of the rooms showed signs of having been left unexpectedly, but helped in no other way.

We searched the larders at my direction

73

because I have known spare bods to be incarcerated in such places purely for convenience and quietness.

There was nothing but a lot of sweet smelling food which took some of the tension off the proceedings and made me feel hungry.

We went into the cellars. There was a feast of wine down there. It would have taken a couple of thirsty monastery inmates and a few years' meditation to swallow that lot.

Nobody was hidden there.

We came out along the passage which I had entered when I had first arrived. In a small room on the left we found Reiz on one bed and Maurer on the other.

Reiz was out, as he had been ever since I'd met him. He looked ghastly.

Maurer was also out. Flat out and reeking of alcohol.

'He is drunk,' Trudi said and shrugged.

I bent and lifted one of his puffed eyelids.

'Not entirely,' I said. 'He's taken a knockout pill as well.'

Maurer still clutched his glass to his stomach as he lay there. The dregs of the glass had spilled out and stained his waistcoat with a new stain on old ones. There were traces of white powder in the wet.

'Someone slipped a powder into his drink,' I said.

The girls looked at me hard. Their looks reminded me that it would not be easy to fool them, should any occasion arise where I might try to.

I showed them the stains and we went out again and to the stable yards where Jason was stamping about and snorting as if dissatisfied with something.

The stalls were empty.

'How many horses should be there?' I asked.

'Three,' Eve said. 'There are six together.'

I went into the stable building. There was a noise from somewhere up the far end. A familiar noise that did not come from a horse.

Round the wall of the end stall I found Jacob sitting in hay, legs stretched out before him, back against the wall, head tipped on to his fat chest.

He was snoring.

A glass lay on its side in the straw near his hand.

The girls came quietly up behind me.

'The same treatment,' I said. 'Not unkind, either.'

'What do you mean?' Eva said.

'If an enemy had got in,' I said, 'his best way would have been to have shot the lot. That way he would be safe. But these men are going to wake up eventually and tell what they saw.'

'The horses have been stolen,' Trudi said.

'There is no sign of violence in the house or here,' I said. 'I don't believe there were any visitors. I think Kate decided to go it alone and get into this castle over the border.'

The girls exchanged glances then.

'She would not go just with two of us,' Trudi said angrily.

'Why not? Five of you wouldn't be much better than two on a job like this. I've said before, you'd be outnumbered, outweighed, outreached and clobbered, by two or by five. I repeat I've said it before but I want you to remember it.'

'She has to get her brother,' Eva said.

'I don't believe her brother's there,' I said. 'I think he's part of the trap to get her.'

Unexpectedly, Eva slung out a hard little hand and smacked me across the face so that it stung quite badly. I hadn't expected such loyalty. In fact, up till then, I had thought Eva had cared less than Trudi.

Trudi smiled quietly as she saw my surprise and hurt.

'You must watch what you say,' she said.

'Then I'll put this quite simply,' I said, 'regardless of your assorted affections for Rudolph, I think that he took my car and left it with the blacksmith. I think that he was not a prisoner yesterday and is not again today.

'He may be being used as a decoy without his knowledge, but it looks pretty smelly to me.

'Somebody laid the trap knowing she would fall for it and try to go alone. Somebody got the message to her not to take me, and so she hasn't. She has gone with the other two.'

'If that is so,' Trudi said, 'where is Anna?'

I had forgotten the flaxen-plaited bundle of buxomity who had first met me in that passage.

'Can she ride?' I asked.

'There were but three horses,' Trudi said.

I went out into the yard then and through a door into the yard where the cars had been. They were still there.

'It is difficult to get a car over the frontier,' Trudi said over my shoulder. 'But a horse you ride through the forest and jump the wire. There are not enough guards to watch the whole frontier and a horse can jump where a man cannot.'

As the horses were all hunters there wasn't any doubt that she was right. They might also have been specially trained for such an expedition.

But that brought the peculiar possibility that this plan to get in the *schloss* was one of long standing.

Which meant that the brother-kidnap story had been nothing to do with the original idea.

'What are you going to do?' Trudi said.

'I am going to see Mort at four o'clock,' I said.

'It will do no good,' Trudi said.

'I'm hungry,' I said. 'You think better on a comfortable stomach.'

'Get something,' Eva said, turning away. 'I will go look for Anna. She must be here.'

Trudi stood in doubt a second or two, then turned towards the house door. I followed her.

I think it was the first time she had not followed me.

Which meant that she was rattled.

She went back into the big kitchen and hauled a ham and cheese out of a larder. She also brought a basket of fancy rolls and loaves.

'Who bakes the bread?' I said.

'Anna,' she replied.

'She must be quite a cook,' I said. 'Where did you get her?'

'She was a pastry girl at what you call the Schnitzelhaus, back along the road.' She started to eat.

'How long back?'

'Three four months.'

'You were lucky,' I said, sampling Anna's skill. 'Now I come to think, there was a fair, fat girl there not unlike Anna.'

'It is her sister. The family owns the place. Father bakes and Mother makes toys for the tourists.'

'They have been there a long time?'

'About three hundred years.' Trudi smiled faintly and went on eating.

That length of time seemed to rule out any idea of collusion with some Red agents no matter from which side of the frontier. Though daughters do not have to grow up with the ideas of their ancestors, my experience is that women have more regard for roots than men.

'Might she have gone back there?' I said.

'I do not think so,' Trudi said. 'But she has a

scooter and goes back there to visit.'

'But not today?'

'She always says when she will go. She is very—what do you say—proper?—like that. Her mother is very strict with the behaviour.'

Which hardly fitted with the picture of the lazy girl I had seen back at the eating house. She had looked as if she cared less than a damn for anything.

But Reiz had got aboard my wagon at that place.

And at that place the following sharpshooters must have found out which boot he had gone in.

The link was therefore too strong to be ignored.

Eva came in and spoke a lot of very quick stuff in German. I caught only words but gathered from them that she had not found Anna.

'What do you say?' I said, when she had run short of breath.

'She is not there,' Eva said.

'Her scooter?' I said.

'Not there.'

'Where was it kept?'

'There is a harness room by the cars,' Eva said. 'She keeps it there.'

'So she has gone home?'

'No. She would have said. She is very—right about things. Very obedient.'

So both these hard-headed girls voted Anna

79

reliable and well behaved, which seemed a good enough recommendation.

'But what if Kate told her to go?' I suggested.

I could see then that neither had thought of this possibility. But in view of what they had said, it was the most likely reason for Anna's disappearance.

Which went even further to showing that Kate was the instigator of this Marie Celeste touch at the lodge.

Eva sat on the table and swung a leg like a man.

'What will you do when you see this Mort?' she said.

'I shall ask him for details of this castle Rudolph is supposed to be in. When I have all that, I shall ask him for the necessary papers to travel over the frontier and have a look round for myself.'

'Like a tourist,' Eva sneered.

'That is the natural way to do it,' I said. 'To succeed in this business you must look insignificant. There is no other way to avoid notice.'

'And then you will cross the frontier?' Trudi said, watching me.

'Naturally.'

'We will go with you,' she said.

'Not like that,' I said. 'The tourist gentleman's women or sisters or whatever are always dressed like women or sisters, not like

80

gun-slinging boys.'

'That is not difficult,' Trudi said. 'But we do not leave the guns.'

'That suits me. But I don't like to be odd man out. Where's the armoury?'

'Two is enough,' Eva said.

'I think I told you, I am a practised shot.'

'We also can shoot.'

'We might not always be so close together.'

'We will try not to lose you.'

'But I shall be alone with Mort,' I said. 'For there is no sense in playing tourist to him. He knows already who I am.'

They considered me as if I were some kind of crook determined to do them down for a pastime. I should say that by that time I was ready to go on with this business because I was fascinated by it.

Also, for some reason, I had taken a toss for Kate.

I hadn't really noticed it until I had found her missing on our return from the ride. The sudden fear that something might have happened to her had caught me such a wallop within that I recognised I was once again on the ski run, going too fast and off balance, heading down a three-in-one grade for the trees.

That's what falling in love always feels like with me.

2

When the girls went to change I had a look

81

round on my own. Kate's bedroom had been one which had been left in a hurry for something, but a second, calmer look seemed to indicate that its disarray was deliberate.

One of the deliberate set pieces which I had seen but the girls hadn't was an automatic lying among the tossed bedclothes.

I picked it out then and made sure nobody was at the door. I snapped out the magazine and it was full of what appeared to be real live shots.

It was a small gun and slipped easily into my pocket.

Back in the hall I pondered another problem. That of a car. I was still working on this when Trudi came back looking most beautiful and feminine.

But I knew that somewhere in that gay print dress there was a gun in a handy position.

'Have you got any papers to get the car across the border?' I asked.

'Yes, but no good. They get stamped at the post, but you have to sign. Catherine would have to sign for the numbers are already there.'

'Then we wouldn't get across with one of them?'

She shook her head.

'It would be better with the horses,' she said quickly.

'There are too many horses already. Besides, tourists don't travel on horseback. We could hire a car.'

'Every one in the town is known. If you hire them the guards hold you for hours questioning why you have hired a car from there and not from them. They suspect at once. They are a rough body of men, I tell you. They do not mean to encourage unwanted visitors. If they have one small thing to suspect that is enough. They will throw you in a cell for days. There is nothing you can do when you are there.'

Which I knew to be very true. The old days of a passport for protection are long dead. With the rising of the Peoples' Freedom Movements all freedom has been killed.

'You mean you need to have a bona fide traveller's car that's come a long way?'

'That is it.'

'But we could drive back West, catch a train, cross the frontier, then hire a car on the other side.'

'No one gets off the train on the other side. You go on to the city, fifty kilometres in.'

'And don't get out again?'

'You speak little German. We are not English. What story is there we could keep to?' She shrugged. 'It is best on the horses where they cannot watch.'

'Suppose Kate has been allowed through? The watch on the fence just didn't do anything when he saw them.'

'What then?'

'The same guard would wait for us. He would act the second time, wouldn't he?'

'Then what way is there?' she said, signs of despair beginning to show.

'Mort,' I said.

'You have great faith in this man, who has no cause to love you for throwing him about the street.'

'I believe he is a business man. To such business comes before discomfort, and certainly before revenge. You must have seen last night that he had some proposition for me.'

She didn't answer that, which seemed to prove its truth.

Eva came in in a blue dress and bolero jacket, very simple, and very startling with red hair.

'There is someone in the forest!' she said. 'Come!'

We went with her upstairs to a room overlooking the front of the house. It was a staff room, plainly furnished. Eva pointed out of the window at the panorama of the firs.

'You will see someone—running.'

I didn't see anyone at all for a second or two. Then I did. Someone was running, dodging to and fro between the trees, running up towards the house.

At that distance it wasn't easy to see anything but a pinkish colour and a dot of gold somewhere.

As it came nearer I made out a naked girl running, the sun, slanting down through the trees, catching her brass gold plaits as they flailed and swung over her shoulders.

'Does she often do that?' I said, surprised.

'There is someone behind,' Eva said. 'Watch.'

There was a movement amongst the trees, as of someone dodging quickly from one tree to another. It did this three times while the girl ran on, increasing speed as she came nearer the house.

The pursuer did not move for a half minute and then appeared again. But this time much nearer. Somehow he had managed to cover the ground without our seeing him at all.

'He is very near!' Trudi said quickly. 'We must get down.'

We fairly ran down the stairs, me in the front as usual.

I got out of the great carved main doorway on to the drive. Ahead of me were rhododendrons and above them the pines.

I ran across the coarse, needled grass to the bushes. Suddenly Anna burst through, running madly, but looking back over her shoulder.

I saw nothing behind her but the shaking leaves she had startled on her plunge through. She looked ahead, saw me and flung her arms out.

She landed in mine and I went back a pace or two to absorb the onrush, half turning to put myself in between her and whoever was in the bush.

As we turned I saw Eva levelling her pistol at

something past me on my left. Anna started babbling gaspingly into my ear, half screaming.

Eva fired. From the corner of my eye I saw something move and shake the dying rhododendrons. Having seen such agitation before I tripped Anna and we both went to the ground with me on top and she wriggling and gasping.

'Hold still! Hold still!' I hissed in her ear.

I saw dirt kick up from where we had just been, then another bullet ploughed in near her head.

Both Trudi and Eva fired into the bush. I don't know with what result, but no more bullets ploughed the ground near us.

Anna struggled still.

'It's all right,' I said.

'It's not all right,' she said, wriggling again. 'The needles tickle my back!'

I held her down, as she acted like an eel on the grass, raised myself slightly and looked back to the bush. Nothing moved there. Trudi was going slowly—very slowly towards it, her gun ready.

From my level I could see more than she could. I could see under the leafy branches of the bushes to the dusty stems and I could see a pair of feet there between two bushes and close to the left-hand stem.

'Stay there,' I whispered.

Trudi stopped.

'Throw yourself sideways!'

She did as she was told, trained to act, I should have said. The shot crashed out of the bushes and missed her by not much. Almost instantaneously Eva fired into the bush.

The feet remained motionless.

Trudi rolled over quickly and ended up by a bush so that the man hiding could not have seen her. But then, no more could she see him.

'I will be killed!' Anna breathed.

'Keep still and it's got to hit me first,' I said.

I worked on the hope that the man did not know me and had no interest; also that for the moment he had to keep his attention on those of the company he knew to be armed.

My situation was unpleasant, but I was covered by the girls' guns. I had no wish to show the gun I had stolen, for even if we won now, I doubted I would be able to have it again.

Eva fired twice into the bush. Trudi tried a slanting shot. There were a lot of wounded leaves and twigs, but nothing else that I saw.

The man in the bush did not fire. It seemed to me he was drawing their fire hoping to exhaust their rounds and then come in with his own.

The girls seemed to have fired blind into the bush, having only an idea of the direction from which the shots down at us had come.

Suddenly it reminded me of the way they had fired into the wood the night before, apparently without seeing anything to fire at.

Now neither were easily scareable and they

hadn't got the jumps so as to fire at nothing but shadows.

I peered back under the bushes. The feet moved aside, slowly, making no sound. It seemed that the man, having failed to get Anna at the beginning, was prepared to hang around doing nothing until an opportunity came again.

Eva started to walk slowly across the grass towards the bushes. At the same time Trudi, who could not have been seen by anyone in the bushes, got up and began to creep along close to them.

They began to converge on the hider, but then I saw the feet begin to withdraw, backing slowly and silently down towards the first trees only a matter of a few feet behind him.

Eva came close by us.

'I can see,' I whispered. 'Drop the gun and go straight on.'

And she did. Without changing her attitude she let the gun fall to the soft needled grass and went on.

I could see legs now, withdrawing as I picked the gun out of the grass.

There was a shot. Eva started upright suddenly as if punched. I fired under the bush at the legs. It was a good gun. I hit the left leg and both collapsed up against a tree.

But Eva staggered a little, then bent double as if winded. Then she collapsed slowly at the knees and fell face down along the grass.

Up by the tree the man had started to limp

away, using hands to drag the upper part of his wounded leg along.

I got up then and went through the dry, rustly bushes. When I came through the thick leaves I saw nobody amongst the vast scene of the straight-up trees. I went to the right so that the scene fanned out and I could see partly behind the nearest trunks.

Nobody there.

I went on, further out to the right and down, making a big arc to bring myself round behind and to the right of where I had seen him reel up against the tree.

And still I saw no one.

The ground was not even between the trees, there were old trenches worn into smooth channels running here and there in the forest, and deep enough to hide a man.

From behind a tree I kept watch on the area, hoping some movement might give him away.

It was interesting to ponder, as I waited, why the man, armed as he was, should have chased a perfectly nude Anna up through the forest to the house.

After all, he could have shot her. He hadn't hesitated to try when I had got her on the lawn, so why not do it before she got near the house?

True she had been dodging amongst the trees, as he had, which made an accurate shot very doubtful. But he could have tried when she was ahead of him.

One puzzle was why he hadn't tried.

Another puzzle was how on earth she had stripped completely naked. Swimming? But this guy was no peeping tom or sex maniac. He was an armed man, and I had seen too many of them round these parts already.

Then some way ahead I saw something rising from the ground. It was the top of a head.

Just in front of it something small appeared, something that glinted in the sun. There was no time to wait and be sure what it was.

He could see part of me as I could part of him. It was to be a slow motion shooting match if I didn't fire first.

When I fired I hoped it wouldn't kill him, but it was a dead shot.

For a second after I fired nothing seemed to happen. Then the head showed itself in full view as it toppled backwards and vanished.

The small glinting object remained lying in the needles.

I waited a while and nothing moved. He made no attempt to reach the gun again.

So I went forward silently over the soft ground until I could see down in the rill.

He lay there on his back, his arms outflung, crooked as if surrendering. I saw Trudi coming quietly on amongst the trees.

She came to a halt on the edge of the dip and looked down at the dead man.

'You are a good shot,' she said.

'I told you,' I said.

I looked back. Eva was leaning against a tree

90

some way back.

'She all right?' I said.

'A bullet hit her holster,' Trudi said, looking down at the man. 'She is bruised. This man is dead.'

'Unfortunately, yes,' I said. 'Now I shan't get my boot lid.'

CHAPTER SIX

1

'What was he doing?' Trudi said.

'Why not ask Anna?' I said. 'He was chasing her, though I could see less sinister reasons for that.'

Trudi looked back past Eva, still leaning against the tree, but there was no sign of the blonde, with or without clothes.

I squatted down beside the dead man. He looked much as he had done when we had seen him not long before, dirty, smudged with honest toil, wearing the same dirty torn shirt and trousers.

'He must have followed us pretty closely after,' I said, looking round. 'There must be a vehicle somewhere about. What was Anna doing? Swimming?'

'There is a lake,' Trudi said. 'Yes. It is possible. We must find her.'

'Surely she just went back to the house for

cover?' I said, curiously.

'That is likely,' Trudi said.

'You mean there's a doubt about it? I thought you found the girl reliable and predictable.'

'Until she was chased by this man,' she said quietly. 'I think he must have had a reason, don't you? He had a gun and he fired it.'

'All this is true,' I said. 'But you are a sharp-eyed lot. I think that you must have detected some sign of inconsistency under her placid front.'

'We did not notice anything. No.'

'Better see if Eva's all right,' I said. 'She's still in pain, by the look of it.'

Trudi went away silently over the quiet ground. I searched the blacksmith's pockets. There were three cigar ends, a couple of smudged bits of torn cloth, four .38 bullets and a piece of paper with a single word in printed characters, 'Molderstein.'

The printing was hurried, uneven, but clear.

The bullets, however, did not fit the gun he had used, which was a .45 automatic.

Now I do a lot of pistol shooting, and I know the bark of a .45 against the crack of the lighter guns, and I could have sworn that the shots fired through the bushes were from a smaller pistol than the one lying by him.

I unclipped the magazine. There was one shot left there.

After stuffing the paper into my pocket I

went back towards the house. Eva was limping along with Trudi ahead of me, though Trudi kept looking back for me.

When I came through the bushes I started hunting round the roughish grass of the lawn. By that time Trudi and Eva were entering the house.

Searching a lawn for a small hole is a task requiring some concentration, and therefore I did not see anyone there until the whisper came.

'Why do you look there?'

I looked up. Anna was standing between two bushes, as nude as before. She watched me unselfconsciously, as if she normally paraded in front of almost strange men in her air suit.

'Do you remember where we fell over?' I said.

'Yes. It was there.'

She pointed to about a yard from where I squatted on my heels. I moved over and had a look at where she pointed. In a half minute I found a score in the dirt and then an oblong hole dug in.

Using my penknife I poked the hole and finally got out a mushed bullet. It was difficult to see from the state of it what the calibre had originally been, but it look like a Continental size, around .30.

The important point was that by no form of collision could a big bullet like a .45 have come to look like this.

I shook the metal blob in my hand and got up.

'Walk with me,' I said. 'Down there.'

'Ja,' she said, and stepped out of the bushes.

'Don't you want to put something on?' I said.

'No. I feel nice like this. You show me where.'

We went between the bushes and over the soft ground between the trees until we could look down on the man sprawling and staring sightlessly at the tops of the trees above him.

'Do you know him?' I said.

'Yes. It is the smith from the village. Why is he dead?'

I have come across quite a few reactions to being presented with a corpse in the course of my career, but never one like this.

She just stared down with wide blue eyes; no shock, no horror, nothing showing but a childish surprise.

Somehow it fitted with the walking around in the nude; as if her feelings were altogether placid, almost innocent.

'Why did he chase you?' I said.

She shook her head slowly.

'That is not the man,' she said.

Which fitted precisely with the different bullet layout. The man who had fired through the bushes had certainly not had a .45.

So there was still somebody loose in the forest who intended Anna no good. Yet she did not seem to think of such a thing.

'Why did the man follow?' I said.

'He came this morning to the house,' she said quietly. 'Not like a visitor, you understand. I saw him creeping outside, watching. He haves the glasses, you know.'

She imitated binoculars by putting her rounded hands to her eyes.

'Had Catherine gone then with the others?'

'Yes. She had gone. I was to go, too. Then I see the man out there and I think 'What are you up to now? I wonder?' and I creep out also and see him going away down through the trees, yes.'

'Yes. Where did you lose your clothes?'

'I do not have any on. I am about to dress when I see the man creeping away. That is how it begins.'

'So you just slipped out starkers and followed.'

'Starkers? Please?'

'Like that. Where did he go?'

'I do not know. I do not go very far, but I look and do not see him anywhere. So I think perhaps it is a burglar and had better go on a little, but I do not see him.'

'Then suddenly I see him in a bush, and he has a gun pointed at me. This is when I run, yes?'

'Yes, indeed. Where is your scooter?'

'The scooter? Ah!'

'Where is it?'

'It is not here.'

95

'I know. But where is it?'

'It is in the woods, you see?'

'Why?'

'That is what she said to do. To go away. To go home. But I forget something. So I go back—'

'You walk back.'

'It is not far, you see, it is only just round and then so I am back.'

'What do you forget?' The present tense is rather catching when there is such a lot of it.

'I forget my purse with the money within, yes? And so I am back most quickly and then when I look in the mirror glass I see that my scooter had made a mark on my skirt. I see that, yes?'

'So you change and then see the man creeping away outside?'

'That is mostly so, yes.'

'And you don't bother to put on any clothes?'

'Not so, yes. I am in a hurry.'

'Or is it perhaps you thought you knew the man?' I said.

She looked very demure—that is as far as one can look so in such attirelessness.

'We are very short of men with Catherine,' she said.

'So you make your own arrangements to meet some?'

'Well, of course, what do you think? A girl with no men is not natural, is it not so?'

We had turned away from the dead smith

96

and now began to walk back towards the house.

The picture was now different, for if oversexed Anna was in the habit of arranging for odd men to be around in secret circumstances then a whole new idea of the state of the lodge was appearing.

The four girl guards might be sharp on the lookout, but Anna, used to love intrigues, could be a good deal cleverer than the watchers.

Certainly they had spoken of her as reliable; so it would seem they did not suspect her as a heel into which the arrow might sink.

'You thought this man was a friend of yours?' I said.

'Oh no. They would not come in the daytime, you see?'

'Yes, I see.'

'Do you know Rudolph?'

'It is her brother?'

'Do you know him?'

She smiled at something, then pulled my arm and we stopped facing each other.

'You know?' she said.

'Know what?' I said.

'This. Verstehen sie?'

She had me round the neck and started kissing me with all lust and no inhibition. With this plump bundle of naked charm in my arms the whole thing was a foregone conclusion.

I could not even think that somewhere nearby the real gunman might still be looking on.

'Anna, listen—'

That was all there was time for in between the big, soft, hot kissing and the wriggling and general overwhelming enthusiasm.

It is a very difficult situation to be in and not give in. It is also very difficult to remember whether I had the intention of holding out, of attending to business.

What happened was that suddenly I felt her feel the stolen gun in my pocket, and one split second later she had snatched it out.

Except that I had her wrist on one side and my arm round her back on the other.

She struggled. She was a very strong girl. A man I would have thrown, but it being a girl I hung on straining to prevail by superior strength.

But she had superior lack of inhibition and she got me in the stomach with her knee and that hurt. So I threw her.

She went down on her back and I still kept her wrist, for she, despite her gymnastics, was still holding the gun.

She was also laughing breathlessly as if this were no more than a romp.

I tried now to get the gun out of her hand and all of a sudden she let it go.

At the same instant she got me round the neck again, shoved her foot against my ankle and brought me down on top of her. Then she started wrestling and kissing and biting and it was all one hell of a big romp in which I faintly

98

realised the gun act had been part of the fun and game.

And some game it was, too, rolling about in the pine needles in Pannish frolic almost made me forget just how I had got there. In the pauses between the gymnastics she asked me to do things in breathless German and then giggled breathlessly and started off again.

The possible man in the forest and all the rest of the possible disasters just fell out of the back of my head.

To a longish-term sophisticate who might on occasion have begun to drop into a routine this was a return to the joys of spring.

With mouthfuls of pine needles, kisses and flaxen plaits and all the other delights so close at hand I had no eyes for anything around, as they say. Nor time, either.

When at last we sat up, laughing and breathless, I looked around vaguely for articles of apparel and oddments.

All were there, spread around, tumbled and tossed, even torn.

But the gun had gone.

The day began to feel cold.

2

She knelt close and started to kiss me again.

'Somebody's been,' I said, holding her.

'It is no matter, yes? It is only me matters, then, yes?'

'In one way yes. In another, no. You don't

want to be shot at again, do you?'

'That is not so, is it?'

'Yes.'

'But why do they not shoot now, before, that is?'

The only reason I could think of (a) he'd gone off with the gun to use somewhere else and (b) it was the staff who had found it.

She started snuggling and biting my ear and I held her back and started to laugh. I couldn't help it. She laughed, too. We were both clutched together laughing like mad when through my tears I saw somebody standing by a tree.

It seemed to me that he was levelling a gun. I could not think why he had waited so long, and there was no time to sort the matter out.

We were rolling and rocking together all sort of mixed up so that the watcher could not have been sure just what belonged to who.

In that confused situation I got my right shoe off, shoved her to the ground and slung the shoe by the toe, as one might a knife.

It got the watcher right in the kisser and he fell back.

I jumped up and over Anna, took about four steps to the man and hit him before he could see straight. One swipe at the side of his bleeding mouth, and another to match with the left and he dropped the gun, half turned and almost fell. He pressed back against the trunk, his head turned sideways to avoid another slam there, but I hit him in the wind instead. He doubled then and looked as if he tried to butt me. I twisted aside and he seemed about to fall on his face.

But he was tough. Instead of falling, he went head first on top of the gun, half buried in the needles.

I got on the back of his neck then. He rolled and threw me, but before he had the gun I got my forearm round his neck and started to throttle him.

He lifted the gun, but it pointed the wrong way and it dropped a little. He panted and grunted, and the gun, still in his grip, touched the ground.

Then a bare foot trod on his wrist suddenly from above and I heard something crack. The man could not cry out because his throttle was stopped by my grip.

But he dropped the gun.

I let him go and shoved him aside on the ground. He rolled over on to his back clutching his wrist.

'It is broke, probably, yes?' Anna said, squatting down beside me as if she were a kid watching a crab in the sand.

I took a good look at the man. His face, twisted, smeared and with needles sticking to the sweat, was difficult to relate with anyone I knew. And yet it did remind me of someone whose face had been almost as dirty—

Maurer's.

I brushed some of the needles off his face. He turned his head, thinking I would hit him again.

'It's Maurer,' I said.

'No it is not,' Anna said. 'Maurer has but a half ear that side.' She pointed to the lobe, and then sat back on her haunches and looked up.

Trudi halted close by, staring down at the group.

Unless you had seen Act One it would have been very difficult to make out from the general scene just what had been going on. Perhaps Trudi didn't try.

'We get him back to the house,' she said and turned and signalled to someone back in the bushes.

Jacob came tramping forward clumsily, as if his knees were on the point of giving way.

'Carry him,' Trudi said, and pointed to the ground.

'I think he's broken his wrist,' I said, looking round for my shoe.

'Maurer will see to that,' Trudi said.

Anna picked up a few of my things and I got the rest and we followed Jacob and Trudi. Jacob carried the man like a sack of coal, his feet dragging the ground behind him.

I found the gun and slipped it back into my pocket. Anna saw and smiled.

'You like that?' she said.

'There are all sorts of things I like to keep by me,' I said and cuddled her against my side as we walked.

She laughed softly.

Throughout the three minutes or so that we had that man on the ground he had not said a solitary word. I had not bothered to put any questions because I guessed he would only lie or pretend no English. Yet it was odd that he had said nothing at all, not even cursed the fate of his broken wrist.

Back in the house he was dumped by the refectory table in the big hall and Jacob went off to get Maurer. Maurer came, bumping against things, pale, but still as drunk as before.

'The man's wrist,' Trudi said. 'See it.'

Maurer almost fell over, then got the wrist, the hand in his left, the forearm in his right. What he did then I don't know but the victim gave a yelp and groan like an animal. It was awful to hear it.

'It is broken,' said Maurer, dropping the limb so that the man groaned again as it fell to the table. 'It will mend. These things do.'

'Get a splint,' Trudi said. 'Fix it.'

The man half started up and grunted several times like a child panting in terror.

'Why bother?' Maurer said, shrugging. 'He does not speak. What matters if he cannot write, either? Forget it.'

'Get a splint!' Trudi said and hit him across the face with her flat hand.

He staggered back and for a moment looked as if he might return the compliment, so I got his arm, twisted a little and shoved him towards the exit where his patient was.

When he had gone I said, 'Has Reiz recovered?'

Trudi shook her head and stood looking at the man at the table. He nursed his broken arm on the table top, stroking it, head bent over it, dirty, dishevelled, abandoned.

Then it occurred to me that this was the second mug that afternoon. First the blacksmith had been made a scapegoat for a shooting he hadn't done, now this man, who didn't look villainous at all, apart from an unfortunate resemblance to Maurer.

I gave him a large brandy from the decanter on the table, though I felt that to withstand Maurer's tender attention he might need a general anaesthetic.

'Get dressed!' Trudi snapped out.

Anna laughed, then winked at me and went out.

'But you said she was reliable,' I pointed out.

'It is you,' Trudi said sharply. 'You are upsetting everything. It all goes wrong since you came.'

'That's rather ungrateful seeing that I have not been out of your sight since I came to this confounded place,' I said. 'Who's Molderstein?'

She started visibly.

'What are you talking about?'

'I found it written down in the blacksmith's

pocket.'

She looked grim then. Her eyes got very cold and sharp as I had seen her when she fired a gun.

'What does it mean?' I said. 'You might as well tell me. I can find it out quickly enough. I have a date soon with Mort, and I am going to keep it.'

She hesitated then, watching the injured man. Maurer came back with his bag. I put the patient's head back and poured the rest of the big brandy into his mouth and some down the sides.

'You'll need that,' I said and put the empty glass down.

He half choked but swallowed all that went in. Maurer dropped the bag. There was some confusion then, for when he bent he tended to fall flat on his face and twice butted the edge of the table.

The second time he did it I went up close to him.

'Molderstein,' I said, close to his ear.

He petrified, slowly, muttered an oath and then went about gathering up his bag with a surprising agility which looked born of sudden, energising fear.

Trudi gave me a hell of a look then went to the table. She took the man's wrist and he let her, but he looked very thoughtfully at Maurer as the drunken physician came forward with his equipment.

'I know how,' Trudi said, challenging him with a look.

Maurer stopped dead.

'Molderstein,' he muttered, and then very loud, 'He said Molderstein!'

'Do your work!' the girl snapped.

The physician trembled very badly as he went about his work. Once or twice the victim grunted, but Trudi steadied the hands of the doctor and made it easier.

When the job was tied up Maurer reached for the decanter but I pushed him aside. The magic word seemed to have penetrated his soaked brain, for he looked at me with something like terror in his eyes.

'Look after the other patient,' I said.

'He is not through yet,' Maurer said.

'How long is he going to be like that?' I said. 'It's been a long time now.'

'One cannot tell. He was exploded. Shock. The brain takes time. Cures itself.' He looked almost desperately at the decanter, then turned away.

'Get back to him,' Trudi said. 'Don't move from there.'

'What of my patients?' he pleaded. 'My patients!'

'They should be relieved you're away,' she said tightly.

He shrugged and tramped out, dragging his feet.

'When do you go?' Trudi said.

'Soon,' I said. 'But I've no clothes. These are getting a bit worn.'

'Not surprising,' she said tautly. 'But they must do for you. There is no other for men.'

'Rudolph. Didn't he keep any spares here?'

'No.'

I looked at the patient. He had his arms on the table, his head lying on them as if asleep after the pain of recent events.

The man was dumb, it seemed, and could be deaf as well. So far this fitted, for he had not spoken and did not seem to have heard when he did not look.

'There are three sufferers,' I said. 'This man, the smith and Reiz. I would guess this chap and the smith were framed into being trapped by us.'

'You are guessing?' Trudi said.

'What else is there? But a man comes here, tries to kill Anna, then deliberately covers himself by leaving two simpletons to face the music. Reiz's case was basically the same. We were to go in, set off the booby trap and blow up with Reiz. You see there is a pattern, a style. Can you think of anyone who might work to set rules like that?'

'It is a popular system over the frontier,' she said drily. 'You frame somebody and are then legally entitled to shoot him, or to forgive somebody who does it for you.'

'Why was the man spying on the house?' I asked. 'You guess now.'

'To see if Catherine was still here.'

'So when he finds she isn't he signals back and they watch the wire along where they guess she will go to cross.'

She made a gesture towards the injured man as he slept.

'Don't bother he will hear,' I said. 'Even if he isn't dead, he's on Catherine's side. You can see what has caused this series of misunderstandings and frames; everybody believes I'm against her.'

She stared, then, but it was so obvious that she just shrugged.

'I'll clean up as well as I can,' I said.

'Use your room from last night.'

'It's really the only one I know,' I said and went out along the broad corridor to the room at the end.

The heavy oak door opened rather like a safe door, so heavy and smooth. I shut it behind me and crossed the sumptuous room to what had once been a dressing room, now a bath.

I washed the needles and earth off me and then got back into my smeared and slightly torn shirt. I made sure my money was still in the back pocket of the trousers as Mort wasn't likely to be cheap.

Then I went back into the bedroom.

Anna was standing by one of the big windows, still undressed, pointing through the vertical bars which guarded them.

The purpose of the iron bars was, I

imagined, to keep people out, not in.

'What are you doing here now?' I said.

'Look,' she said pointing and smiling. 'That key out there in the grass, you see that? It is the door key. I locked the door and threw the key out there. That is clever, yes?'

She threw her arms round my neck again.

'No!' I said. 'Not clever at all!'

CHAPTER SEVEN

1

I got Anna's arms from my neck and pushed her back. She was laughing with high glee and no small anticipation, which shone in her expression and restlessness.

'What's the idea of this?'

'What do you think then?' she said and looked askance in exaggerated surprise.

'Are they the only keys?'

'Of course. I would not throw away if there was some others would I, for what then?'

I shoved her aside and went to the door. It looked hewn from the solid black oak. It didn't even rumble when I bumped it, the whole fitted so well into the frame.

The bars over the windows were firm, even in the adjoining bathroom. It was an all-purpose guest wing, to keep one safe.

'You're a nut,' I said, coming back.

109

'I am getting very impatient,' she said. 'Come to bed.'

'I am going to get out of here,' I said. 'Are there any other keys? Who's the housekeeper?'

She shrugged.

'You?'

She curtsied, and started to laugh again. I just avoided a sudden lusty attack by twisting aside and sitting in a big carved chair.

'Don't you like me again?' she said, pouting. 'What's the matter, then?'

'I like you very much,' I said, 'and nothing would give me greater pleasure than to you-know-what with you, but not now. This is not the time.'

'Any time is good time—' she began, trying to get on my knee. 'Why do you hold me off?'

I suppose that when one falls into a set-up of intrigue and double-cross one might expect any sort of stalling device to prevent one getting ahead in clearing things up.

But I had not imagined one like Anna.

Suddenly I let her get on my knee. She started to make the most of it and I held her tightly so that she was almost still.

'This is your idea?' I said.

'It is a very good idea, yes?' She bit my ear.

'Nobody told you to do it?'

She straightened.

'You do not think I would do that? Who would tell me?'

'That's it. Who would?'

'I think you talk foolish.'

'You like Catherine?'

'She is lovely.'

'She is your friend?'

'Yes, yes, yes,' she said wriggling impatiently. 'This is nothing to do with us, no. Kiss me hard.'

'Do you think I am Catherine's enemy?'

'Oh, no, you are too nice. Kiss me hard.'

It seemed politic. Pleasantly so.

'I want to get out of here,' I said.

'No, no, no, no, no!' she said, doing her best to make me stop wanting to.

Once again I had to hold her still.

'If we don't get out I'm afraid something will happen to Catherine,' I said.

'You cannot stop that, it is not worth to try.' She bit my ear again and it became very difficult to hold her still.

'Why not worth trying, Anna?' I said, struggling. 'What will happen to her?'

'Look, it is nothing,' she said beginning to sulk a little at the apparent failure of her wiles.

'But I want to know. Catherine has been very kind to me, Anna.'

'She will not hurt. It is arranged she will not hurt.'

'So you do know something about it?'

'Kiss me hard!'

It was impossible to avoid it. I was near smothered. Apart from an obvious enjoyment I came to the conclusion that she was trying to

111

sex me out of wanting to know what she knew.

Until then I really did not think she knew anything.

And yet she had been chased by the man with a gun.

Certain events and their pressures had rather pushed this fact into the background of my mind.

'Why will Catherine not be hurt?' I said, when released.

'Because it is money, only money. She can buy herself back. It is nothing. She has plenty—'

'You mean this is a ransom job?'

'Job? What is job? Why do you not kiss me?'

It hadn't occurred to me to be a ransom frame. I had thought all along of a political racket of some sort. But if it was ransom it was surely easier to deal with. Ransomeers don't usually operate in large numbers.

But then, Kate had organised her guard of four some time back. Had it been ransom she had suspected it would have been easier to get out of the district, get police protection—

Unless she had suspected that her brother Rudolph was behind it.

The need to get out of that room became pressing if Catherine had been kidnapped, because suddenly it occurred to me that plain ransom wasn't enough.

It was enough, perhaps, to stuff Anna with, but to me it seemed that Rudolph would gain much more than a ransom sum if Catherine never came back.

And deaths are not particularly recorded in some iron curtain layouts.

Some thought and investigation would be necessary to find a way out of that pair of rooms and the decision I had to make was whether to try and stave off Anna while I did it, or please her first and hope it wouldn't take too long. Which is never the way I like to do things of that nature.

While wrestling with this problem I heard someone on the other side of the door.

'Why have you locked the door? Open! Open now!'

It was Trudi's voice. I shoved Anna off my lap and went to the door.

'Someone's locked me in,' I said. 'Is the key out there?'

'There is no key here.'

'None here either, but I saw a key lying out on the grass by one of these windows. The end one. That could be it.'

'Jacob!' Trudi called. 'Get round. Look for a key under the guest window West.'

'It is a pity we are interrupt,' Anna whispered, hugging my arm.

I was relieved she took it so pleasantly. But when Jacob got outside the window and found no key, I thought differently.

I went to the window. Jacob was moving around, staring at the ground, shifting grass

113

with the side of his boot and shaking his head.

'Someone must have tooken it,' said Anna, hugging my arm tighter.

'Who's with you?' I said, pretty angrily.

'You are, darling.'

I disengaged her and went back to the door.

'He can't find it,' I said. 'Can he break the door?'

There was no answer.

'No,' Trudi said, after a while. 'It will do for you to stay.'

And that was that. Nobody in the whole of that exotic dump trusted me in any way whatever.

'But Anna is here,' I said, seizing on a poor straw.

'Anna!' Trudi sounded sharp as a sword.

'We're locked in together, you see,' I shouted through the mighty panels.

I heard Anna stifling laughter behind me.

Trudi went off into a fearful stream of German, which really sounded as if she were whipping somebody. I saw Anna go on laughing but clap her hands over her ears and make a pantomime of fear and alarm.

And then came the shock. Another voice. A man's voice, sharp, short. Even I understood the German.

'Keep your back turned. I have a gun here. Drop yours to the floor.'

It seemed that Trudi hesitated for there was a flat crack of what sounded like a Luger and

114

an answering rattle of the door. The shot had been to miss and to warn.

I heard Trudi's gun thud on the carpeted floor.

'Good. Now march!'

The muffled sounds of movement through the thick door died away. I turned round. Anna had stopped laughing.

'Who was that?' I said.

'It was not good,' she said, and turned quickly to the windows.

'Do you know who it was?' I got her arm, for a change.

Before she could answer we heard shouting from outside the open window. It was a man giving orders.

'It's more than one,' I said. 'Can't you guess?'

She couldn't guess or didn't want to. Suddenly she was frightened and got a silk bedcover and draped it round her and tied it in the middle. It was deft, skilful, so unyokel that I remember holding back to watch it.

'You've done that before,' I said.

'My mother makes dresses, too,' she said.

The jollity had gone. She was taut, then, as she followed me over to the window.

By putting my head through and close to the bars I could see along the gateway to the yard the cars were kept in. There was no movement to be seen, but the voices were barking now and again.

She came close to listen.

'Tell me what he says,' I whispered.

She did nothing for a bit. The air was still and the voices carried.

'He is asking,' she said quietly, 'where is the staff? It is Trudi—no, it is Eva. She says—no, she does not know, but she says it otherwise.'

'What sort of otherwise?'

'Like you say stuff it?' she said, quite innocently. 'That is what the English say, I think—He is angry. He says—' She broke off to listen again.

'What does he say?'

'He says he will skin them. Both girls.'

I did not bother to ask how they did that round these parts, for they had new inventions all the time, and the newer they invent tortures the further they go back.

'Seriously?' I said.

'With whips,' she said.

'Flay is the word wanted,' I said, and moved from the window. 'We've got to get out of here.'

I thought it highly likely they wouldn't know we were locked in that room; that they had come across Trudi without giving time to find that she was talking to someone on the other side of the door.

If that were not the case they would have done something about establishing contact with us, such as chucking a bomb through the window. Instead Trudi's captor had just walked away with her.

'Do you know any way out of this room?' I asked.

'There is no way because I throw the key.'

'Who took the key?'

She shrugged.

'You weren't surprised when it had gone.'

'I see a man out there.'

'When?'

'When you kiss me once.'

'Did you know him?'

'I did not have time. It was too exciting.'

The shouting came again. We both listened.

'What's he say?'

'He say he will burn the house down.'

'It's an empty threat,' I said cheerfully. 'It's worth too much. I hope.'

2

There was a pause in the threats from without. I took a very fine look round the suite but there was no easy way out.

The only possible way seemed to be to pick the door lock, a job which I have done before, but at which I do not excel.

What gave me the idea was an old-fashioned button-hook I found lying on a vast chest over by the bathroom door.

By shoving the hook round the flat of a brass window catch and levering carefully, I straightened the hook from a sharp crook into a curved right angle.

Thus armed I started poking about in the

lock and trying to remember what a class picklock had once told me.

'Can you do that?' she whispered, coming up behind me.

'I don't know,' I said, poking.

I stopped as I heard uncertain footsteps coming along the passage outside. A chair grunched as the walker fell against it and there was a mumbled curse.

A moment later there was a thump against the door and a breathless grunt.

'Damn and blast, damn and blast!' we heard the drunken voice through the panels. 'Six men. All armed—six—' Those words were clear, then the door rumbled and we heard the mumbling, drunken voice going away again.

'Six,' I said. 'All armed. That's a nice round number. Maurer can't be as drunk as we thought.'

There came the crack of a pistol, and then Maurer cried out. A second or so later we heard him tumble to the floor, then there was a brief silence.

A voice called out in the passage, giving a short, sharp order. Footsteps went quickly away. They certainly weren't Maurer's.

'He has been shot!' she whispered.

We heard a breathless muttering and half groan coming from outside, then gasps and a little clink.

Millimetre by millimetre a key was pushed under the door.

118

'It is the key!' she hissed in my ear.

I picked it up and tried it. The key worked quite silently.

We heard feet marching down the corridor again.

'Pick him up,' a man ordered.

There came a fumbling and grunting from outside, then footfalls drew away again. They had taken Maurer.

'Open the door!' she breathed making a snatch for the handle.

I caught her wrist and she became still. With my other hand I turned the key to lock again. As I did it, the handle began to move from the other side. It turned fully and stayed like that while, I guessed, somebody tried the door. We heard nothing. The handle slowly returned to stillness.

She stood aside as I pushed her slightly, then turned the key to unlock. I pulled the door open silently.

A man was in the act of walking away from it. I got him round the neck, pulled hard so that his spine almost cracked and dragged him on his heels back into the bedroom. When I had him inside she shut the door and relocked it.

While she did that I got the man face down across the bed, his arm locked up behind him, my knee in his neck. In that position he was locked solid, so solid that he didn't try to shout.

'See if he's got a gun,' I said.

She searched and found some kind of

Russian machine with which I was not familiar, but it was like a Luger enough not to be one.

I was about to ask a question and eased the pressure on him a little to let him speak. He misunderstood.

He struggled for an instant with all his strength and snapped his neck like a stalk. It was a very stupid thing to do.

He went like a sack and I let go.

'He is dead,' she said, with an air of quiet interest.

'Something like it,' I said.

I turned him over on the bed and searched his pockets.

'I know him,' she said musingly. 'He came with Rudolph once, but he is Magyar. There was a fight. He nearly kills Rudolph.'

'Does Rudolph fight with the lower orders?' I was surprised after what I had heard of his celestial habits.

'I think he have some—hold, is it?'

'Do you know who is likely to be with this man?'

'From the other side,' she said at once.

'Why have they come here when Catherine has gone?'

'Perhaps they are to rob.'

And then I remembered.

'My God, no!' I said. 'The man Reiz! They tried to kill him before. He must be important to them—'

But if Reiz was all they wanted, why were the

girls being interrogated? Reiz was lying flat out in a room, open to all and unguarded since Maurer had been wandering in the corridor.

And Maurer, drunk or not, had shoved the key under the door, the only key, which he must have got from out on the grass.

Quite suddenly Maurer did not seem quite so drunk as he had appeared to me. Obviously he had taken some risk outside the door and been shot for it. Perhaps he hadn't expected it, but he had taken the risk.

The dead captive had not been much use, except to tell us that his companions were likely to be invaders.

I opened the door and looked out. The richly furnished corridor was empty, but I could hear men's voices somewhere ahead, probably, I thought, in the hall.

'I'm going to find what's happened to Reiz,' I said in a whisper.

'I come with you,' Anna said. 'I do not wish to be killed all alone.'

It was quite matter of fact. I was getting to like her, but I couldn't see what she would be like if we did get within range of a death chop. As I couldn't shake her off without some noise and delay, it was better to risk it and take her.

'Keep behind, then,' I said and checked the magazine of the Russian pistol. It was full but for one, which had probably gone into Maurer.

We crept along to the hall. I peered round the edge of the door, but the place was empty.

The voices came from somewhere right on the other side of the vast room, down one of the passages leading off.

I led a way along the left-hand wall of the hall past big black carved chairs and massive sideboards.

As I passed one of these I saw, too late, a man step forward from behind a piece of huge furniture and raise a club in his hand.

But it seemed he had not seen Anna.

Anna jumped on his back, her arms round him. He reeled back under the unexpected attack and I got him clunk under the jaw with the pistol barrel. A foul shot but he went down like a sack, with Anna on top.

She was up in a flash. I checked the man was out.

'Know him?' I whispered.

She shook her head. We straightened and went on, more watchful now.

The voices were still faintly audible but intermittent. We could not hear enough to tell what was going on.

We got to the passage leading down to the stable yard and, on the way, the improvised sick room.

And when we got here, it was empty. The two beds were made up, tidy, uncreased.

'What has happened to Reiz?' she hissed in my ear.

'Well, the invaders haven't taken him. They wouldn't bother to clean up like this.'

I looked around, but there was no sign of Maurer's bag of empty bottles and glasses. The whole place was swept clean.

There had been four able people in the house up to the time of the invasion: Trudi, Eva, Jacob and—Maurer who had been more able than we had ever thought.

Unless something had happened to sober him up.

That was more likely. The girls had swept him clean, too, at least as far as possible in the time.

'It must have been the girls and Jacob who took him,' I said.

She was at the door listening, but now she turned back.

'Then they must have known somebody would come,' she said.

'Or was it a precaution because they were leaving?' I said. 'Either way, whoever did it is with us, and the invaders haven't found him. That was what the questioning was about.'

I went back to the door. There was silence in the house. The talking men must have been too far away for us to hear.

As the original threatening shouts had stopped I thought that for the time being the girls were not being molested, but now that it seemed the helpless Reiz might be safe, they were the next consideration.

I went into the stable yard. There were restless movements of horses in the stables, but

123

normal ones, not the sounds of animals being startled by strangers.

She followed me as I went to the yard gate and looked along the side of the house. I saw nobody.

It was from somewhere on this side the voices had been coming. Further on there was a terrace to which I knew a range of french windows led out. As we crept along the soft grass we began to hear odd snatches of talk, but still indistinct.

The men were now talking quietly, usually a sign they feel they have a lot of time. If they had, for what were they waiting?

We stood awhile not far from the break-in to the terrace.

'Can you understand?' I whispered.

'It is difficult,' she answered, frowning and cocking her head. 'They must be in a room. The girls must be there, too!'

'Why?'

'They say of how they will use the cold water interrogation—'

I heard a laugh break the talking.

'Then he says, "We will see that you talk for you cannot swim with your arms tied to a plank".'

'So they must be in that room, and this is really the opening of the inquisition. The man who shouted was an underling, perhaps.... What is it they want to know?'

She shrugged, shook her head quickly and

124

went on listening. Suddenly she touched my arm and looked very surprised.

'They ask where is Catherine!' she said.

'Catherine! Then they haven't got her!'

Since coming back that day we had assumed Catherine and her two girls had gone across the frontier of their own free will, but these men, being here and pressing for an answer, obviously knew she hadn't.

Equally obviously, it seemed to me, they had been waiting for her and when she hadn't come, they had come to fetch her.

But there was another point. I didn't see how Trudi and Eva could know where Catherine was, so even if they broke under torture they still couldn't speak.

I crept forward then to the reveal which broke back into the terrace side wall. I tapped Anna's arm to make her stay. At the corner I peered round to the line of white-painted, arc-topped french windows. A pair stood open and inside I could see something moving. A foot swinging impatiently.

Getting down below the top of the balustrade I moved along a little until I could see a little more of the room.

There were four men, all facing the part of the room I could not see. Undoubtedly the part was where the girls were for I heard a question from one of the men.

'Where is your mistress? You have two minutes.'

There was no answer, and no one spoke after that.

Had I been a hero of some sort, I might have vaulted the balustrade, rushed in, held the men up with my Russian pistol, and got the girls out.

But it occurred to me that such men would not leave just the one rearguard out in the hall, and a game of check, double check could help no one but the enemy.

It was good that I decided to hold back at least for the two minutes because towards the end of that time, a door behind the men opened and a man came in.

He bellowed out something which I did not understand at all in the language he used, but by instinct I knew he was saying that our victim had been found lying ko'd in the hall.

One man got up and went with him. I noticed he had a gun ready. The other three also seemed to get guns in their hands from nowhere.

This was the moment to get Anna out of it and make plans later.

I backed up to the wall again.

'Come on!' I said. 'Into the thicket behind the stable yard. It's as safe as any!'

I took her hand and we ran. We got into the jungle of wild trees and bushes as I heard somebody come out into the stable yard and shout an order.

And at that moment, a hand gripped my gun

wrist. I turned from Anna and looked into the face grinning close to mine.

'If Mahomet does not come, the mountain must,' said Mort.

CHAPTER EIGHT

1

I looked at the huge man, his face pushed close to mine. It was like an orang-utan, grinning.

Anna made a movement, I thought to shoot him with a gun she produced from her drapes. I got her wrist and held the weapon to one side. It was instinct more than anything, a feeling that Mort would help. Not a very startling instinct, since during that day I had determined that Mort would help me, whether he liked it or not.

'You have some difficulty here,' Mort said, nodding his head towards the house.

'I have several difficulties,' I said, letting Anna's arm go as she relaxed. 'About six. They are all in the house. They have two captives I want.'

'It is my business to help with difficulties,' he said, grinning amiably. 'But there is the question of the recompense.'

'Name the price. I'll get it out somehow.'

'I have your word, then?' he said, searchingly.

'You know I'm a crook?'

He shrugged.

'Five thousand pounds sterling,' he said.

'What do I do? Invest in it you, or something? There are restrictions—'

'You give me your word. I will get the money out.'

I could see that he would take my word. I could also guess what might happen if I broke it. A man like Mort obviously had international enforcing arrangements.

'What can you give for five thousand?' I said. 'I must know what I'm buying.'

He looked towards the house, then, peering between the leaves of the small trees, 'There are six, you say?'

'Armed and, I am sorry to say, fully alerted.'

'Yes. I heard some commotions when I waited for you.'

'The commotions seem to have died down,' I said. 'Which is always a bad sign.'

'One does not bother with signs, but with facts,' Mort said, still watching the house. 'There are six men in the house and several doors standing open.'

'They could think I was still inside,' I said, and told him how we had laid out the guard in the dining hall.

He spoke with Anna, asking questions very quickly in her language. I gleaned from the exchange that it was details of the house he was getting.

While the talk went on I watched the house. We had a long, slant view of the terrace and I saw the shadow of somebody moving along by the balustrade but did not see the person.

'Do you think these men have come from the other side?' I said.

'For certain,' he said, frowning so that his thick black brows met. 'Tell me what happens all this afternoon.'

I told him from the time Anna had been chased through the forest.

'Ja,' he said. 'That would fit the pattern.'

He looked at Anna, but did not say anything to her.

'It is necessary to get these men,' he said.

'I was thinking the same. It just needs a careful plan in which we don't get shot.'

'That would be a desirable detail,' he said, looking towards the house again. 'What do you have in mind?'

'There are two girls being held. That means at least one man must be there to guard them. As there was a double guard outside the room—one outside, one up in the hall, they might even use two guards on the girls, a guard and a cover for the guard.'

'Suggests military practice, yes. It fits with the pattern. They will be searching the house. One way is always to make a diversion outside to bring them out of the house, then shoot.'

'I hardly think they'd fall for that,' I said. 'They would be outside now if your idea was

129

right for them.'

'Ja. We consider all points, all possibilities, then we are not likely to be taken with surprise.'

'Think of a surprise, then,' I said. 'We might get the angle. They expect some men—they don't know how many, remember—they've had no means of finding out. They expect them to be armed. They expect them to be enemies. They expect to have to fight.'

'All this is true but advances nowhere,' said Mort.

'But yes,' Anna said quickly, 'for if they find a man who is none of these things they will not know which to do.'

Mort made a lugubrious face. It was like a rubber mask.

'But they would have seen you,' he argued. 'With Anna in the forest. Did the man not shoot and you threw her to the ground to save her? Was that not what you said?'

'But they haven't seen you, have they?'

'That is for certain,' he said. 'I am not a bloody fool, as you would say.'

'Okay, then. I will walk in. You will hide. They'll not know you're there but they'll suspect there will be a lot of men behind me for me to risk walking in.'

He began to shake with silent laughter.

'Where do you think you are, in the pavilion at Lord's or somewhere?' he said. 'These men shoot and then find out later.'

'Men work on behaviour patterns,' I said. 'If puzzled they don't act at once. They wonder what you're supposed to be doing. That causes a pause.'

He shrugged again. I thought he was going to say goodbye, because he looked as faithless in my project as that.

'The girl has a gun,' he said. 'One must remember there are plenty guns around this house. It has been organised for a siege. It is best not to think a man is unarmed because he has dropped a gun. What do you have?'

'I've got this Russian Luger-type which has more bullets than the others I have handled here.'

'I am well fitted,' he said.

'Right. What I shall do is walk in the french window along there. You cover me and listen to what happens. I may need cover pretty quickly.'

'You will not go!' Anna said, grabbing my arm. 'You will be shot and then I—'

'I don't intend to get shot,' I said, and took her grip off, quite gently for me. 'That's the whole idea. If we try and escape while those men are in there, we will all get shot. That's my belief.'

'Okay then,' Mort said, bringing a forty-five out of his pocket.

I like a forty-five to cover me. It's a stopper. It stops a man right where he is, blasts him to a standstill where smaller bores can let him still run on.

131

We came out of cover and along the side of the house. We watched everywhere, in the yard, over the forest, everywhere that someone might be hiding and saw nobody.

I was still sure the men were all inside, and that none were separated from the main body since the finding of the kayo'd guard.

I left Mort and Anna near the corner of the terrace, turned out into the woods and then came back towards the terrace openly, hands in pockets, strolling.

The inside of the room I had seen into seemed dark by comparison with the brilliant late afternoon sun, and the people I saw were shadows only to begin with.

I mounted the terrace steps. My heart thumped in my ears so that I almost didn't hear the short bark of a startled order from inside the room.

Then I saw a man appear full length in the windows, a gun in his hand, pointing at me.

He bellowed something that sounded like an order. I turned and looked over my shoulder as if thinking he was commanding somebody behind me. Then I shrugged and strolled on.

'Where's Catherine?' I said, trying to be cheerful.

'Halt! Halt!' the man shouted.

'Who—me?' I said shuffling to a half stop. 'You must be making a mistake. I'm a guest in this house. Are you rehearsing for amateur dramatics or something?'

I heard a startled laugh from one of the girls back in the room. The man glanced over his shoulder in a fury.

He couldn't have been more obliging to one of my practice in the noble art of offence.

I got his gun wrist, pushed it out, swung him with the suddenness of the movement and, as he turned back, got his left arm and kept him turning till I got an arm tight under his throat in my favourite locking device.

He had not anticipated a tiny movement of it. My casual advance had done its work better than I would have betted on.

His gun wrist was still in my hold as I held him locked against me.

'Drop it,' I said. 'It's no good now.'

It clattered to the stone paving. I saw three men moving in the room, the blue glint of pistols, but none could fire without hitting the Kapitan or whatever he was.

One or two orders were shouted and a man went to the door I had seen used before.

I let the Kapitan go very suddenly, in surprise he toppled forward headfirst into the room. I shoved him in the seat with my flat foot and he fairly hurtled across and butted the man at the door. It was a thunderous meeting. They staggered together in a mixed up bundle of clawing arms and tripping legs, fell over a chair and crashed to the ground.

One of the two other men tried a shot as I ducked and got my gun out. He missed and got the edge of the stonework round the windows. The shot screamed away and I got a good one in at him, right through the shoulder.

The other man got in behind the two girls who sat tied in chairs. He made too risky a shot there, but he could have shot me so I got back in behind the reveal of the opening.

That meant the two men on the floor rolled under cover behind a table hefty enough to stop any bullet but an anti-tanker.

First surprise being over the battle was on. The initial stage won, the second stage now opening seemed a dead loss.

But there came a shot from somewhere behind me and over to the left of the balustrade. It had a thick bark and I knew it was Mort's forty-five.

There was a bellow of pain from behind the table. A moment later I saw one of the two men—the Kapitan—go on all fours to the man behind the girls.

Mort, not lacking in quick approval of the situation, had fired from the balustrade right under the table.

That meant two down, two to play from balk behind the girls, and at least one guard outside the room.

And by then I had to realise the kayo'd guard must surely be on his feet again, which meant two outside the room.

The shots would have drawn them, but which way?

Two shots were fired from behind the girls. The bullets came out through the window, but didn't seem to have any aim.

I took a quick look round towards the trees in case they had been intended as a signal to someone out in the forest. I saw nobody.

The door of the room crashed open and a man appeared. He made an easy shot as he stopped there, holding the door handle in a moment of indecision, wondering what was happening, where to shoot.

I got him in the leg. He collapsed, dropped his pistol, and rolled over on the carpet hugging his knee to his chest and bawling.

As he went I recognised it was the unfortunate gentleman whom I had already dusted with the pistol barrel. It was not his luckiest day.

Which meant there was still one outside the room.

There was a quick answer to my shooting of the man at the door, in fact several. Shots fairly peppered the stone and wood near me and splinters of wood and stone flew off. Before I ducked I got a three-inch wood splinter in the ear and it stung so I thought for a moment I had been shot by one of the screaming bullets ricochetting away from the building work.

But the men remained behind the girls. And there came a dead and almost accurate shot as I peered round to confirm the position.

It was a bad position. One that looked as if it

135

would be very difficult to solve.

2

Throughout my stay in this exotic establishment I had, with male assurance, badly underestimated the girls. And one in particular, who had led me into thinking of her as just a bit more than a blonde bundle of buxom bedware.

At the time I thought her waiting out amid the trees, covered forwardly by Mort, but I should have known by then she couldn't wait for anything.

The door had been left wide open by the man I had shot away from it. As I was watching for shots from behind the captives I saw a movement in the open doorway only from the corner of my eye.

But I saw enough to know somebody had crossed the opening and gained cover on the side nearest me.

From which position he would be able to see and fire at me where I stood round the reveal of the window.

So I had to back out of it and lose my command of the room. Which meant that, apart from enemy losses, we were back at square one with the enemy in command of the room and the captives.

Even as I started to back a shot banged the stonework by my middle and screamed off unpleasantly close by.

Another shot came, but it sounded different.

Indeed it was, for I saw the man behind the doorway appear. But on his knees, with his head looking up at the ceiling. He seemed to be trying to do a knee walk before he collapsed in a heap, rolled over and lay very still.

And then in the doorway, and out of range of the two remaining men in the room, I saw darling Anna, her gun in her hand, creeping forward to the opening.

Thus in a split second, by her courage in entering the house alone, the tables were reversed yet again. We were in command then.

Behind the girls or not, the two remaining fit men could not hope to hold out.

'Okay, Mort!' I called. 'Come in. They're surrounded.'

His big shape came up over the balustrade but in a position where no shot from the two men could touch him. It was clear he knew this sort of game to the omega, but even he looked surprised at the turn-about.

I spoke in through the windows.

'We have two guns here and one at the door covering your escape,' I said. 'You haven't a chance and we have plenty of time. From the count it looks like two dead, two wounded and only you left. Throw your guns on to the table and you won't be hurt. You have thirty seconds.'

It sounded like a quiz game, and from the sudden relief of the situation I had a strong feeling to laugh.

'They could have tried the old game of threatening to shoot the girls first, but if they did, there would be no escape at all from death and one does not threaten where there is only the certainty of death as the comeback.

But when the solution came it was part ideological.

One gun was thrown on to the table. Then there was a shot.

I was on the point of going in then, and did not realise for a moment what had happened.

It was very simple. One man had thrown in the gun, and the other, the Kapitan, had shot the traitor. But in transferring his angry attention he had left himself open.

Trudi suddenly rocked herself on the chair and brought it over sideways. It left the sole remaining man completely exposed to me.

I went to the window.

'Drop it!'

I could see he meant to fight it out yet if he could, but Anna rattled out some spitting German from the doorway.

He saw her for the first time, then shrugged. The tension went from him suddenly as if his props had collapsed. He just dropped the gun on the carpet and raised his hands to shoulder height.

I felt I could do with a stiffish drink.

We got the girls undone.

'What did you do with the doctor?' I asked

138

the Kapitan.

'He is lock up.'

'Get him. Your friends need his care, whatever it is.'

Mort jammed a gun in the man's back and drove him out of the room. He came back almost immediately with Maurer following vaguely behind.

'You weren't shot?' I said, blankly.

'It was sad,' Maurer said. 'In my pocket I have a flat flask of Scotch. Bang! The shot hit. All gone. Scotch!' He looked as if he might cry and touched his hip pocket. 'Such a waste.'

'Do what you can for this lot,' I said, indicating the wounded.

'Just one moment, please, thank you,' Maurer said. 'Who pays? This is big work. One, two—three—no, two. And already I have fixed Reiz—'

'You will be paid,' Trudi said. 'Attend them and make sure they don't get away from you. Is that clear?'

He shrugged miserably.

'I will get my bag, but it is too much. It is a whole surgery I do. Reiz and the broken arm. Now these—I do not know. I need nurses, operating theatre—'

'Get on,' I said.

He turned hopefully at the doorway.

'A drink,' he said. 'I have suffered much—'

Trudi shoved him out. Mort got the surrendered man by the scruff of the neck and crammed him down into a chair. Mort took a chair, spun it on one leg then set it backwards in front of the captive. He sat astride the seat and rested his ape's arms on the back.

'Now, you tell me where you come from, who is there,' he said and smiled pleasantly.

The man did not answer. Mort hit him with such a crack I felt pain myself almost. The fellow rocked in the chair. Mort pulled him upright.

'Now, you tell me of your own free will,' he said.

Still the man said nothing. Mort hit him again even harder than before and grabbed him effortlessly as it looked as if the fellow would topple off the chair. He was dragged upright.

'Now, you tell me,' said Mort.

Again no. Again a terrific blow, again a pull to the upright like setting up a falling ninepin.

'Cut his ear off,' said Anna. 'I will get a knife.'

'That is a good idea,' said Mort, happily. 'Yes, fetch the knife.'

I began to feel slightly ill and shocked that my warm Anna could have made such a cold suggestion. I don't know the Continental mind too well, and often when I have thought, 'Oh no, they wouldn't do a cold-blooded thing like that!' they have gone ahead and done it and laughed like mad as well.

I felt very uneasy. Mort just sat grinning at

140

the victim and did not ask him any more questions. The Kapitan's face shone with sweat.

Anna came back with a large pointed kitchen knife.

'It is sharp?' said Mort.

She grabbed a handful of the prisoner's hair, pulled it up then sliced it off with a deft swing of the knife.

'The hell with this!' I remember muttering to myself, forgetting completely that this man and his fellows had been using the same sort of effects on the two girls not long before. That's the sort of clunk I am.

Anna offered Mort the knife.

'No, no,' Mort said. 'You are used to cutting up the meat for the pies. Please!' He opened his hand towards the prisoner as if offering a rare gift.

'Very good,' said Anna and moved round behind the captive.

I saw the man swallow and lick his lips.

'I tell,' he said.

She let the edge of the knife rest on his ear.

'Don't move your head,' she said.

He sat rigid, sweat running down his face.

'I tell,' he repeated.

'Don't move your head,' said Mort, smiling in a friendly fashion. 'You tell. Yes?'

'Molderstein,' the man said, breathing the magic name I had found in the blacksmith's pocket.

'Don't move your head,' said Mort again. 'You are sure?'

'Molderstein,' the man repeated, blinking as the sweat ran into his eyes.

'Operating from where?' Mort said, bringing a squashed packet of cigarettes from his pocket.

'From Bayen.'

'You came from there?'

'Last night.'

'But it is not many kilometres,' Mort objected.

'We stay night in the forest.'

In began to dawn on my stupid brain that Mort was deliberately using English so that I could follow every twist of it. It was one of the things that made me begin to realise that he was a good deal more than he appeared to be.

'Which man shot at the girl who holds the knife?' I said.

He sat rigid.

'Myself,' he said in a strangled voice and looked as if he would faint.

Anna started to laugh and the knife joggled on the Kapitan's ear. I reached out and lifted her arm. The prisoner looked as if he would faint and slumped in the chair.

'You left the other two so that they got caught for what you did?' I said.

He nodded. Mort laughed and knocked him clean out of the chair without getting up himself.

'It is bad for innocent men to be dead for you,' said Mort.

The Kapitan rolled over and sat up, shaking his head.

'It was not innocent,' he said thickly and spat out some blood. 'The smith was paid. He was a fool. He should not have hidden from you. He was scared. That was it.'

'What about the man who cannot speak?' I asked.

He stared up blankly.

'I know no such man,' he said.

He remained sitting on the floor. Mort smiled benignly at him and he almost shrank.

I went out of the room and signalled Trudi to follow me.

'Where is Reiz?' I said when we were outside.

She said nothing for Maurer was coming along the passage carrying his bag. He almost fell over going into the room so I guessed he had taken some small fortification.

We went through into the hall and I took a long drink from a carafe. Trudi had some water.

'Where did you fix him?' I said. 'Reiz?'

'A cellar beneath. It has a thick door.'

'He ought to have a real doctor. He's been out a long time.'

She shrugged.

'It is not for us to decide it.'

'Tell me about Molderstein. It's a code name

143

for something?'

'The organisation that comes over and—' she shrugged again, '—takes people.'

'They came to get Catherine but she went too soon?'

'That would seem to be it.'

'Is that what you were expecting all along? The reason for your being armed?'

She just nodded.

Mort came into the hall with Anna. I feared the worst.

'Where is the Kapitan?' I said.

'The doctor is looking after him,' said Mort.

I thought it best not to ask more.

'We've got to get to Bayen,' I said.

He lit a cigarette and smoked slowly, turning the smoke on his tongue with his mouth open.

'We can, of course, get there, yes?' he said, gesturing with the cigarette as stirring a pudding. 'But the chances of getting back? That is the interesting factor.'

'You know the ways and means,' I said.

'Ja. Forsooth, as your Royal Family says. Forsooth indeed. I know the ways and the means and each one ends with a—' He drew a finger across his hairy throat and ended with an upward flick of it. 'You understand, it is not our country. The disadvantage is considerable.'

'It must be done.'

He did some more smoke rolling on his tongue. The blue looked solid till he blew it out.

144

'It is certain she has gone there?' he said. 'Certain?'

'Where else would she go?' I asked.

'There are all sorts of places in the world,' he said. 'You are here and all round there are ways to go. Three hundred sixty degrees and you choose one. Then the further you go the wider the degree gets and so you can bend. Why should we *go* in one of three hundred sixty ways just for an idea?'

He sat down on a chair, backwards again and rolled some more smoke round his mouth.

'You say she has gone that way,' he went on. 'Now why do you think so? Because you have the idea. But ideas do not come from nowhere. They come from people. What people give you the idea she has gone that way?'

His eyes were very narrow as he rolled more smoke. But they were not so narrow that I did not see them slide towards Trudi.

And of course, he was right. Where else had I got that idea?

CHAPTER NINE

1

I could see what Mort meant. Trudi had spread the idea that Catherine had gone over the border to the castle, and it was now a question of deciding which side she was really on.

145

Whether, in fact, she was after rescuing Kate, or whether she was out to get Kate finally caught and having us trapped with her.

Trudi was a difficult girl to assess, apparently so cold, and yet in fact, quite hot. And if she could be hot in the bedroom her feelings could be as inflammable at all times.

Yet which way now? Which side did she really burn for? It was almost impossible to find out. It was an urgent unanswerable problem which was suddenly solved by a forgotten item.

Eva came in.

'Reiz has regained consciousness,' she said.

I don't think we said anything, but just gave up our various positions and went across to Eva. She turned and led us into the cellars and the sick Reiz. He had been calling, it seemed, and when we went in he was thirstily drinking from a cup.

He put it down and looked at me.

'You have seen me before,' I said.

He nodded.

'Why did you choose my boot to hide in?' I said.

'They were behind me. I had to hide, to get away, to lead them off.'

'To lead them off Rudolph?'

'Yes.'

'Where is he?'

'I do not know. He got the train, back where I got your car. It slows past the crossing below

146

here. He was to jump then. I do not know if he did.'

'He meant to come here?'

'Yes.'

'He didn't get here.'

He turned on the pillow so that his face went to the wall.

'Then they have won after all. He did not jump the train. They must have stopped him.'

'Why do they want him?'

'They want both, she and him. They worked together, brother and sister, getting people across. What you call Scarlet Pimpernel? That kind of thing. Now they need such a one themselves.'

'She has gone to get him back. She had two girls with her.'

He turned on to his back again.

'Madness! They will be waiting!' he said.

'At the *schloss?*'

'That is the place they all go. No one gets out, yet it is so open. One does not suspect.'

He was exhausted and closed his eyes again.

It seemed that Trudi was on the right side.

'You will arrange for me to cross the frontier?' I said to Mort.

'We shall go in a party, which will seem innocent,' he said. 'Tell the blonde to get dressed like the others. She will not look good, rolled up in a curtain.'

We waited in the hall. Maurer reported from his hospital. Three dead, two wounded, one tied to a chair.

'Lock yourself in with them,' Trudi said sharply.

'But wine—I must have wine—' Maurer started to protest.

'Go!' said Trudi. 'Jacob will be with you.'

Maurer shambled away muttering. I looked to Mort.

'Don't you want to ask the Kapitan any questions about the castle?' I said.

'No, no, no, no,' he said lighting one of his strong cigarettes. 'I know it well. It is a tourist place. Bus tour.'

'Okay. If you know.' I looked round as Anna came in dressed like a Gretchen doll. 'You know, Mort, Rudolph did jump that train. He dumped my car with the blacksmith. I think he jumped the train, hid, and then after the explosion in the wood, came to meet Reiz and finding the marks of the fire, thought him dead.

'He went on, found the car and hid it because it was a clue to the meeting of Reiz and himself. He didn't want his pursuers to be led so close to this house.'

Mort rolled smoke with his tongue, then shrugged.

'Anything is possible.' He looked around the three girls. 'All are now ready. We go.'

'How?'

'With the car. The big car you came to me yesterday with.'

'That means crossing the frontier by road.'

'We shall use finesse, mon ami,' he said.

He stuck his cigarette in his mouth and brought a bulging wad from his pocket. They were ten dollar bills. He stripped off twenty, folded them together and put them in his right-hand trouser pocket. The rest he put back in his hip pocket.

'This will go on the expenses which you will pay me,' he said and smiled benignly.

We went out to the Impala.

'The village where we cross has no bar, you see,' he said. 'Instead of the barrier pole, they shoot.' He laughed. 'But they know me, and my dollars. You will see.'

We started off. I was to see all right, but I could also see a bit farther than the crossing of the frontier into the curtain country.

I could see to the return journey—if there was one—and the unwillingness of the guards to let us out again, specially if we had Rudolph and Kate with us.

Only, as I drove along, I realised that I didn't believe Rudloph had been snatched at all. I thought he was still safe on the right side of the border.

Mort sat in front with me with the three girls in the back. With the hood down it looked a real live tourist get up with the courier and guide sitting in the front to point out the beauties of the scene.

We drove through the forest to the top of the hill and looked down a winding road beyond the fringe of the trees. Below, nestling in amongst scattered trees were a few cottages and the silver ribbon of a railway line crossing the road just a few yards our side of the village.

There were crossing bars at the rail, upright and open as we came down.

'It is because of the rail crossing there are no bars on the road. It would be dangerous confusion,' Mort said.

He was smiling and at ease. I began to wonder if we would get across or whether he was going to sell us to the guards down there.

As we came down, our scene began to act. Mort started to bawl out and point to distant mountains. He knew the guide book by heart. The girls, playing up as if used to this sort of charade, asked a battery of questions.

We came into the village, crossed the rail and headed for the men gathered in the roadway. Our side just looked round, the others barred the way with waving of arms and sloping of rifles which could be quickly raised.

We passed the Austrians who only looked at the girls. The armed men gathered round as we stopped.

'I take them just to see the fireworks at Bayen,' said Mort genially. 'Three hours only.' He handed over the roll of dollar bills.

The money disappeared very quickly as if the recipient was practised in sleight of hand. He signalled and we were let through.

'You know them well,' I said.

'One buys one's way so far,' said Mort and shrugged. 'But you will see a car come out soon and follow.'

We drove on the winding road through thickening woods.

'There we have it,' he said. 'About four hundred metres behind now.'

I looked in the mirror and saw a car following some way back.

'That rail line,' I said. 'It seems to run at right angles with the one which crosses the frontier in the town.'

'Indeed, indeed,' Mort said. 'There is a junction in the town and this line branches off South as you see.'

'The fireworks? Was that a gag?' I said.

'No, it is a feature for tourists in the castle. Big set piece and rockets and flaming tributes to the Red Army and such. Very impressive. Victory at Stalingrad. The Reds are always advertising their strength to the small countries they own.'

He laughed.

'One kilometre now,' he said, 'then you will see Bayen upon the little hill. Very beautiful. Turrets and fairy tale roofs.' He laughed again.

As prophesied, we came in sight of the *schloss* on a hill rising out of a sea of trees. In the gathering dusk they looked purple and the castle quite black.

We came round the last bend in the road and saw the black gates ahead, but to the right there was a large car park filled with cars.

'It will be best always to park so that no one will get in the way,' Mort said.

Anna leant forward.

'Over there by the road. You see. The fence is weak there and propped up with wood pieces. Somebody has been through there and broken it, ja?'

Her eyes were sharper than I had thought, but she was on the other side of the car from me and I could not see the detail for another few yards. When I did I headed for it.

A man came up and stopped us for the fee. Mort paid and waved away the change.

It all seemed so ordinary, like an outing to Runnymede.

But such an exterior is a wonderful disguise for sinister matters as we of the Western world have begun to learn, if only slowly.

We stopped the Chev by the broken fence and got out and went across the drawbridge. The gate had arrow-slitted guardhouses on either side commanding the bridge.

Inside there was a series of tiered lawns leading up to the castle proper. There were a good many people wandering about. On the second tier there were the set pieces and rocket stands waiting for the display.

Beyond that the way up was barred by the fireworks and I could not see how on earth we were to get anywhere to get contact with Kate, even if she had got this far.

Mort was carrying out his part as the guide to the life.

We went to a stand and had mugs of lager and boiled sausages and sat under the trees to play out the part like the rest of the tourists.

There were a number of uniformed men around, in amongst the crowd, but I couldn't tell whether they were on duty in the castle grounds or visitors come for the night out.

In many adventures into which my evil life has led me I don't remember anything so frustrating as this jolly scene of relaxation and apparent innocence. I would sooner have had bats flying out of the castle and maidens screaming from the turrets. You could recognise the baddies that way. Certainly not this way.

And then in the moving panorama of people laughing and parading in the dusk I saw Kate.

2

It was a momentary revelation. I saw her and then the moving crowd passed across the view and she was gone.

'She is there,' I said.

'You are sure?' Mort mumbled, eating his way along a foot of boiled sausage. 'Alone?'

'No. With a man.'

'Let us go and look nearer at the set pieces,' Trudi said, touching Eva's shoulder as she got up.

The two girls went off and became lost in the

human whirlpool. Anna sat with me, giggling over a mug of lager.

'She has not been taken yet,' Anna whispered. 'That man has been to our house. That man behind them as they walk. He has been to the house.'

I saw Kate again talking with a man, but the man Anna pointed out stood behind the couple.

'Who is he?' I said.

'I know only his name, Strauss. He comes to our house and eats and meets other men. It is a society or something.'

And then I realised she meant her family house, the Schnitzelhaus, as I had christened it.

The house, in fact, where all this had started for me. Where Reiz had fled, by way of my boot, from an organisation which loosed off rounds of automatic fire in the hope of stopping him.

And he was there now, watching Kate.

This meant one obvious line which connected up most things.

Strauss joined the Schnitzelhaus through the holes in my boot to Bayen. I had no doubt whatever he belonged to this side of affairs, not ours.

He was watching Kate, which must have meant that he watched her hoping that she would bring someone else to her side. If not, he would have taken her before.

'Who is the man with her?' I said under

154

cover of taking a draught.

'I cannot see,' Anna said, smiling at me. 'When they move a little. Then.'

It was heartening to be with a couple of experts like Mort and Anna, people who acted their parts so well nobody near us would ever have seen anything to suspect us of spying here.

I went up to the stall and got more lagers. They weren't serving them to the tables, perhaps as a gesture against servility, or the equality of all but non-party members. It was good because I was able to move around and get different angles on the situation in the vast courtyard.

The situation was depressing. There were quite a few uniformed attendants or guards, or whatever they were, scattered around the mighty gateway and mingling with the crowd.

I brought the tray of mugs back to the table.

'It's a hedgehog defence,' I said to Mort.

He shrugged.

'The man is Rudolph,' said Anna, smiling as she took her beer.

'Good God!' I said. 'You don't say!'

'Yes, it is Rudolph, the man.'

Well, if Strauss was watching both the people he most wanted to get there, for what other person could he be waiting?

And then came the cold feeling that he might be waiting for me.

His organisation must know that I had driven the original car with Reiz in the boot,

155

had been a part of the snatch which we had made in the bombed forest.

They could also know by now that their expedition to the hunting lodge had ended with disastrous results for the visiting side.

None of these things would leave me as a very safe representative on the other side. In fact, if they got the lot of us now, the thorn in their side, the pimpernel thorn, would be cauterised.

I would be no more than a regretful note to the British Ambassador telling of my sad death falling in some falls or down some inaccessible mountain crack, from either of which my corpse could never be retrieved. Just, perhaps, a pair of shoes lying by the river path somewhere.

One thing, Strauss obviously didn't know me or something would have been done by now. He could be waiting for someone who would know me.

And then one other thought occurred.

We had been brought into the country by Mort's bribe, with no papers, so nobody need apologise anyway.

The question of what had happened to my belongings didn't seem important at that stage. Even if I'd had them they wouldn't conceivably help much.

The first problem, anyway, was how we were all to get out of the castle, and supposing we all got together, it would make a large party. Kate,

Rudolph, Anna, Trudi, Eva, Mort, me, and possibly the other two girls who had come with Kate. I couldn't even remember their names.

We were all armed, but so were the rest of the uniformed gentlemen hanging around the place. On spec it seemed a shooting match would be the least desirable confrontation.

I saw Mort grinning at me across the iron table.

'You lead,' he said. 'We follow.'

'I don't know the damned place,' I said.

He grinned.

'I have to be careful of my reputation as a guide,' he said. 'I do not wish to lose my business because of one customer.'

'So?'

'So when you go, I follow, but I pretend to chase,' he said. 'The subtle difference, comprenez?'

'And how in hell do I persuade everybody to follow me?' I said.

'It is getting dark,' he said, looking at the sky. 'I think the fireworks will begin soon.'

The pyrotechnics might distract the guards a while, but surely not that much. Assuming Strauss to be in some sort of charge, knowing Kate and Rudolph to be inside the grounds, it wasn't likely they would be let out.

It really wasn't likely that anybody would be let out.

The whole situation seemed plain hopeless. Three of us together at the table and six

157

scattered amongst the moving crowd with no means of getting them together without making the whole thing obvious.

I began to wonder why I'd come. After all, it was no business of mine and really Kate and her girls had spent most of their time not trusting me to be in the game anyway.

It was depression brought on by inactivity.

What was happening amongst the girls I did not know, but as the crowd parted a moment or two, I saw Trudi and Eva laughing as they passed Kate, apparently without seeing her.

After that, Kate looked towards me and contact was established. It was something, although we passed no signal at all that might have been spotted.

Obviously, Kate having found Rudolph would have gone had there been a way out. The fact they stayed there still showed they knew there wasn't; or what one existed wasn't worth the gamble.

Mort went to get more beer. I shifted my chair to get closer to Anna and whisper in her ear. Also to see directly to the main gates.

One or two people came in through the opening, but the uniformed guards kept suspiciously away from it, trying not to be too noticeable amongst the crowd.

Mort banged the mugs down.

'You think?' he said. 'But I see you get nowhere.'

'One can only use what's here,' I said.

'Fireworks, people. I don't see much you can do with that.'

A band started brassing away somewhere up the terraces and the people became more stable in their wandering pattern expecting something to start soon, and turning their attention towards the firework plateau.

Looks between myself and Kate connected often now, as if she understood exactly what was in the wind and was ready to have a go, whatever chance it had.

Trudi and Eva stood nearby her but gave no sign of recognition. We were therefore beginning to be linked, which began to solve one pressing problem.

'The two girls who came with her,' I said to Anna. 'Do you see them?'

'They have not come in. They would not,' she said firmly. 'If you wish to escape you must have somebody on the outside to help. That is certain.'

If that was the case and the two were somewhere outside it might be of value or not. What did help was that it made two less to contact inside. In fact it meant all the isolated characters in that impending fun fair were linked by eye if nothing else.

'I have the men by the gate,' Mort said, rolling smoke with his tongue. 'The nearest ones are four. They all have pistols and clubs.'

Clubs you can dodge if quick, but pistols need something in between them and you, something to absorb the bullet. Another person is the best, perhaps, but not easy to come by dependably.

And yet—

The idea glimmered while the music got louder. It got brighter. I fingered the Luger-type pistol in my pocket.

'If nothing happens,' I said, 'those border guards will let us back?'

Mort nodded.

'The payment was enough for that. But if anything happens, no. And if we do not get back before the change over, then no, also.'

He grinned and rolled smoke.

'But,' he went on, 'it is a long way from here to the village.'

'Two inches is a long way if it's the thickness of the prison door,' I said, uselessly. 'When do the fireworks start? We've had fifty-nine Red Army songs already.'

Mort shrugged. Anna laughed and snuggled up to my arm.

'You do not like music, but it is very good for soothing the nerves.'

'Then I could do with a lot more,' I said.

The music ended and as I tautened up for the opening of the display, it started off again. It was by then pretty dark and the lanterns under the trees were all ablaze. My guess was that for the full enjoyment of the great display these would be switched off. It would mean both advantage and difficulty for us.

160

But I was betting that the display would provide a lot of light, but of a rather weird kind.

I was glad to see that Kate and her brother had moved nearer our table. Both were talking busily, even gaily together.

Trudi and Eva came back to our table to drink their beer. They showed keen interest in the coming display, none whatever in us. They were also showing keen interest in boys sprinkled amid the crowd and laughing to each other about them. There was a good deal of eyeflashing going on and I began to feel anxious in case it brought a hopeful swain to hamper our future activities.

It was very hot under the lanterns but most of the heat I felt was coming out through my skin. What I hoped to do would be a near miracle if it came off, even for a competition shot like me.

In fact, it damned near never came off at all.

The band worked itself up into a frenzy of martial glory. Some of the uniforms started to stand to attention. The lanterns flickered in the trees and I tensed up like a strained knot.

But the music had one of those endless ends, when you kept thinking the last roll, the last tarr-arra, was really the last, instead of which comes another. So this lot blew and banged and clashed time after time, playing Wagner with the hiccups.

Then it ended. The conductor turned and bowed and people cheered.

And then the lights went out. I stood up as I could hear all other hitherto squatting people had done.

There was a roar and a whizz, a line of streaks went up into the sky, and then great fountains of coloured lights burst, enormous plumes in the night.

CHAPTER TEN

1

The initial rise of a rocket is slow and then it accelerates very fast. From where I was under a tree I could see the left-hand line of rocket chutes without a head in between. The first rush of rockets into the sky had given way to a glowing wall of multicoloured fireballs popping in weird fountain designs.

'Get the others close by,' I told Mort.

He ambled off as a loud sighing 'Oooo' greeted a wall of golden rain sparkling like sequins with red and green balls.

There was a comforting racket of bangs and cracks accompanying the display and the more of these the better if the wild scheme I had devised was going to come off.

The Luger-looking gun which I had won was of the type where, if the trigger is kept depressed the gun fires on like a machine gun. This one held nine shots, of which six were left.

162

I took careful aim at the centre rocket chute and got the stance dead right. The Roman candles went on banging and popping and showering golden rain and coloured balls into the air. There was a lot of noise, shouting and laughter and excited calls to look.

I dropped my arm and several times raised it and took aim, practising until I had the movements right.

But the rockets were not yet. A couple of honks in asbestos suits outlined in fireworks had a kind of slogging match in the smoke with sparks flying when they hit.

Then I saw a letter-off coming up beside the rocket chutes, a dim figure in the smoky glare from the combatants.

I glanced round me and saw the others close by then, Mort in command, watching me.

The first lot of rockets had been quick firing from the chutes, obviously with some automatic firing device.

The fighters faded into dim red outlines and ambled off in the smoke. The first rocket hissed and started up.

I fired ahead of it to hit the body above the fire tail. The crack of the gun was lost in the roar from the people and the crackling of some banging Catherine wheels that were starting to spin.

Another rocket rose. I fired a second shot holding the trigger down for two. This time it was a dead hit and the rocket exploded in a wild mass of golden sparkling fire, darting plumes of smoke and glaring colours shooting in all directions.

Cries and shouts of alarm rose above the crackling of the wheels.

The third rocket started and I got it with two shots dead where it had to go. The thing started up, a fiery tail then tipped over and headed right down towards the crowd.

They ran, and so did we. The panic was on. I got Anna's wrist and the others came after. There was a banging and cracking, a yelling and the terrifying sound of many feet running in madness over the turf.

We rushed down to the great gate, outlined in jazzing colours from the wildly zooming rocket on the ground and the wheels up on the terrace.

The guards were swamped in the crowd bursting through the gate. We were almost driven off our feet by the stampede, a rush of panic made worse by the constant flare and searing bursts of flame from the broken rocket darting around on the ground behind us.

We streamed over the bridge and on the other side began to slow and disperse a bit, people coming to their senses now they realised they were safe from burning.

I saw Mort's big figure moving amongst them, nowhere near us but heading round down to the park.

There were a lot of people standing about,

breathlessly talking about the inexplicable disasters and we went on down, Anna holding my hand tightly.

Through the gate I saw the lights switched on again and some sort of calming voice bellowed out through a tannoy. It grew fainter as we went down to the park and got to the Chev. The others were there then, seven of them cramming into the big car. All were there.

We joined in. The car faced the castle up the hill and now I saw men running down the slope towards the car park and I knew very well they were guards.

'Kick it down,' Mort said.

I did. We shot ahead right through the temporary fence which burst up like the end of a rocket flight and some of it came whirring down into the car.

We swung round on to the road as a guard came right ahead of us holding up a hand and a pistol. Mort fired over the side and we hit him with the wing of the car as he dropped his gun and reeled away, spinning.

A lot of cracks came from behind, mixed with shouting, the bellowing of the tannoy and the general uproar of frightened people who don't know what was going on.

We had got clear of Bayen, but how clear we were likely to get after that was a matter for a wild guess. The signal would be out ahead of us, and the chase would be on from behind.

'Isn't there another road?' I said, my foot flat

down on the floor.

'There's a forest track,' Kate said from the pack in the rear seat. 'But you can't get all the way. We could ditch the car there and run.'

'We'll do that if we have to,' I said. 'So far the road's empty.'

But not for long. Very soon Kate called from the back.

'Lights behind!'

I saw the signs in the mirror. Not lights, in fact yet, but the glare of lights on the trees beyond the bends behind us.

At this time the clock said a hundred and thirty k.p.h. and any more would mean running out of road with these bends. I even had to ease because the big Chev, overloaded as it was, started rolling like a ship with the idiotic speed we were taking the bends.

The glare of lights grew brighter behind. Doubtless they had some more suitable vehicle for such road chasing than we.

'In one minute the village,' Mort said. 'It will be no good to try and rush it. They have automatic weapons. We should be drilled like drain covers.'

I eased my foot.

'What then?' I said.

The lights behind grew brighter. Through the tall stalks of the trees on the bend ahead I saw twinkling yellow lights from the village on the frontier.

'Everything will be watched,' Mort said,

tapping on the door sill with his thick hand. 'We have to decide where they will not look.'

'Or where they look and see nothing unusual,' Anna said, crushed up in between Mort and myself with Trudi sitting on Mort.

'We could shoot it out,' Trudi said.

'They won't shoot women,' Kate said from the rear.

'They will shoot anybody,' said Mort, without emotion. 'These men ahead are dead set for trouble. They let us through. At all costs they must stop us getting out or they themselves could be shot. At leisure.'

This was painfully true. Another painful truth was that we were rushing headlong for disaster and couldn't think of anything to avoid it. We needed time.

The lights ahead became clearer, the trees thinner. The lights behind were glaring, but still not in sight.

I took the sensible way, turned off the road and with the lights out, bumped and rolled in amongst the trees, steering roughly by the village lights behind the tree trunks.

I kept on going until we were deep in from the road and lurched to a stop on one of the old, smoothed-over ditches.

'This will give a few minutes to think,' I said and got out.

Car lights flickered and ran by on the road, two lots, heading into the village.

Some of the others got out. I couldn't be

sure who. In the darkness they were just shadows, reassuring shadows but no more. The biggest one came up as if Mort could see in the dark.

'You thought of that rocket device,' he said. 'Surely this should be easy for you.' He chuckled.

'They'll make a sweep through this forest when they know we've slipped the road,' I said.

'You have an idea?' he said.

'An idea based on a wild chance,' I said. 'It is that, to sweep the forest they will weaken the guard at the post in the village.'

'Then we go in, shoot the holding force and escape,' said Mort. 'But do you forget, if they seek us, they will not use any force within sight of our own guards, so the block will be on his side of the village, where nothing will be seen by our men.'

And then Rudolph came in. I didn't realise who it was speaking at first, having almost forgotten there was a third man.

'There is a train in twenty minutes,' he said.

'But it runs on the other side of the border,' I said.

'Just a few yards south of the road the rail is on the border. It is the border,' said Rudolph. 'There is an old ox road crossing there.'

'Surely not open?' I said.

'It is wired,' Kate said.

'You mean the car could bust through?' I said.

'It could, yes.'

'But how to get the car to the crossing?' I said. Rudolph stood close to me and pointed so that I could see his finger against the yellow lights of the village.

'It is exactly there,' he said. 'When the train comes the noise is great, and the men must watch to make sure nobody gets on or off. Such jumping has become quite a sport about here.'

'I see. A diversion of interest,' I said, and then turned as a new set of lights appeared flickering between the trees. 'They're coming back to look.'

'I would give myself up,' Mort said. 'Say that you held me at gunpoint and so on and so forth. But I think I would be shot if I did. Also they have unpleasant ways of asking questions.'

'Not you, but I,' said Rudolph.

'No!' Kate said quickly.

'But yes, sister,' Rudolph said. 'Listen to me. In eighteen minutes now, the train. We try to get the car over to the crossing where there will be a guard. We stop where he does not see. Very well. I go into the village through the side ways, give myself up. I call that the party is escaping down the line, then they must go to see. They cannot lose you. That is important. The train begins to come. You have many guns. You start firing. They will run then.

'The train comes. It is noisy, this train, a freight steamer, blast and chuff, whistle and clatter. There is nothing like noise to confuse.

169

Now you have shooting, the train, shouts, excitement. The diversion lets me have a chance to go, because they will run for you.

'You drive through, then, but you must go fast to make it. The wiring is strong. If you tried it without the diversion, you would be shot from either side where the guard stays.'

'How many in the guard at the ox crossing?'

'Two. Automatic rifles, grenades. I have experienced them before.'

'Not you, Rudi!' Kate said again.

'It is my turn, sister. Your friend here has done much for us. But for him we would not have this chance now.'

And suddenly she agreed.

'You should be covered,' she said. 'It is too risky alone.'

'Get the car away,' Rudolph said. 'If you cannot get it through the trees you will not get over the crossing that way. Try.'

The fellow knew the layout and the habits of the guards and the types they were. I knew nothing of these things, could only guess, so it was sensible to do what he said.

He had, after all, been running the frontier for some time and knew if the risk was worth it. But I didn't like it.

I got in the car alone. The speed would have to be walking pace, picking a way in the dark and trying not to get ditched somewhere.

Mort walked ahead, testing the ground. The engine murmured, nobody made a sound as I picked the way between the trees, sometimes scraping the sides the way was so narrow.

We got almost clear of the trees and then Mort stopped and came back to me. The others stood round, listening to the quiet night and faint, shouted orders from the village.

The guards were all alerted. In the starlight I could see the yellow gravel of the raised ox road leading to a fence. There were two men there, tense, rifles in their hands.

I got out of the car.

'Rudolph,' I whispered. 'Stay a minute.'

The motor was off. The night was quiet but far off I heard the drone of a locomotive whistle and the steady, fast chuffing of a steamer.

'It is the train,' Rudolph said. 'I have to get into the village. Quickly!'

'The best way is to take these guards by surprise,' I said. 'That way we stay together.'

'But they are alerted, you can see! There is no surprising them now. If they suspect anything they call the rest from the village. They keep many men.'

'Mort,' I said, 'you get on the other side of the track into the slope there, creep up on the guard and wait. Rudolph, you do the same this side. You are both armed, make sure you get them when you get my signal.'

'We can never get near enough in time,' Rudolph said. 'They will hear, shoot before we can, and the train is not near enough to cover us.'

'I'll cover you,' I said.

'How so?' said Mort.

'I shall walk towards them right along the middle of the track. They won't expect that. Surprise will make them hesitate. It always does. It makes them doubt. They will think I must be innocent, not someone trying to escape. Under cover of my noise, you get up there.

'Kate, get in the car with the others. Be ready, as soon as you hear a shot, start up, rush up this slope and along the track. We'll run back to you and get aboard so you can get a good run at the wire. Okay?'

'Okay,' Kate said.

She got into the car with the other girls. It was a fearsome vehicle then, for each girl had a gun, though Lord knows—and me—a pistol in the dark is not the best of weapons. You need something that will spray and have a chance of hitting, like the guards' automatic rifles.

Mort went across the grass grown track, keeping to the tufts under the trees until he dropped down and vanished into the grass slope the other side.

Rudolph started to creep on our side. Everything was quite quiet but for the distant train.

I got up on to the track and started to walk along, making sure to tread on the noisy stones and not on the grass tufts.

Ahead of me I saw the guards' faces, pale blobs in the starlight as they turned. To the right, beyond the yellow lights of the cottages, I saw a red column of firelit smoke from the oncoming train.

I walked on, heart thumping to the tramp of my shoes.

One guard stood forward, gun set at me.

'Halt!'

Naturally I halted. He shouted a lot of stuff at me that I couldn't understand.

'My Aunt Nelly's got locked in the lavatory,' I called back. 'Her two friends are also in difficulty, one stuck to the seat.'

Without turning his head the challenger rattled out something to his companion. Neither understood English, I am grateful to say.

The challenger bawled at me again, and I understood it to mean approach a bit nearer. So I did.

The locomotive was getting loud now, exhaust roaring in the night and I could hear the clatter and rattle of the freight wagons behind it. I whistled.

Mort fired from the left-hand side. The rearmost guard threw up his rifle and staggered back, turning before he fell.

Rudolph fired from the right, twice.

And missed.

My whole being froze up as the guard's gun sprayed flame down across me and into the slope where Rudolph was. I snatched out the Luger-type and fired. I got the guard in the side. He half turned to spray me with bullets but I fired again and his shots dug into the ground. He went down the slope, rolling.

The train was roaring now, the pillar of firelit smoke rising into the sky a quarter mile on my right. I slid down the slope to Rudolph. He was groaning and I felt wet blood as I tried to pull him up.

I saw the car drive up the slope, swing round on to the track and come racing like a big cat along the track above us.

It stopped and I saw Mort standing in front of it. He shouted, but the train was too loud for me to hear.

Shots started from the direction of the village. A lot of shots, and I heard some pop into the earth of the slope where I was.

We were nearer the village than I had realised.

I hauled Rudolph up the slope. He was like a sack.

Mort gave me a hand and we got him up together and just tumbled him over the side into the car. We followed, as the engine roared softly against the row the train made.

Two bullets or more ripped into the body of the car.

'Get going for Christ's sake!' I shouted.

I knew why Kate hesitated. She wanted to know about Rudolph but she suddenly realised our time was almost up, and shoved her foot down.

We surged forward at the pole-and-wire barrier. It looked impregnable in the starlight. To the right the huge iron-studded locomotive roared down towards the crossing, belching fire above and in between the tracks. It was some sight. One I never wish to see again.

The car struck and shivered right through, grinding almost to a standstill.

But it went on pushing. Instead of bursting the barrier it shoved it aside, scraping the car side as, relieved of the drag, the Chev leapt forward right across the front of that bloody locomotive. Whether any shots were fired at us I don't know but I was hit in the hand at some time and didn't even notice.

The locomotive was too interesting.

It was huge, right above us and tearing into the side where I was. The car, racing forward, must have taken it near the rear end for it was pushed right over and to the side of the tracks, shooting us all out in a scrambling heap of twisted limbs right down a grassy slope into Austria.

I remember the tearing row of the brakes clapping on right down the train, and then, gratefully, seeing it stop right across the ox track, blocking off any hope the pursuers might have had of snatching us from the friendly ground.

We got up and ran, scrambling, Mort

175

carrying the slightly built Rudolph on his shoulders.

2

I stayed quite a month at the hunting lodge. How Mort and the others fixed the dead and wounded, removed the signs of the two-day war and kept it all dead quiet, I don't know. It's not my business.

But before I went I came to realise that the raider snatchers had been either disbanded or sent somewhere else, because in the next month, instead of the usual amount of snatchings, there were none at all.

'It is finished for them for now,' Mort said, in one of his talkative visits. 'The gang is bust. If there is to be more political kidnap it will be somewhere else but here.'

'I never saw the man with the broken arm again,' I said. 'What happened to him?'

'He got the sack,' said Mort. 'He was my assistant, spy, you would say. I like them dumb, but not that bloody dumb, as you would say.' He laughed and rolled smoke round his tongue.

'One thing puzzles me about the Continental mind,' I said. 'Why did they leave Rudolph and Kate free like that?'

'Free?' said Mort. 'You must be joking. It was an extension of the bait game. They have him, he brings her, she brings you and me. If it had not been for the fireworks, not one of us would have got out of there any more. It would have been very sad. It was fortunate that no sign of a link between the unlucky pair and ourselves showed up. Obviously, they waited for a sign, an attempt to pass a message, something, but there was nothing.

'By the time we all got away, it was too late for them.' He rolled smoke round his tongue. 'It was very interesting, I thought.'

'Very,' I said, looking at my healed-up hand.

'You will not forget our financial arrangements?' he said.